SHORT CUTS

Thriller Publishing Group, Inc.

"I love the way this man writes! I adore his style. There is something about it that makes me feel as if I'm someplace I'm not supposed to be, seeing things I'm not supposed to see and that is so delicious."
REBECCA FORESTER, USA TODAY BESTSELLING AUTHOR

This book "is creative and captivating. It features bold characters, witty dialogue, exotic locations, and non-stop action. The pacing is spot-on, a solid combination of intrigue, suspense, and eroticism. A first-rate thriller, this book is damnably hard to put down. It's a tremendous read."
FOREWORD REVIEWS

"A terrifying, gripping cross between James Patterson and John Grisham. Jagger has created a truly killer thriller."
J.A. KONRATH, INTERNATIONAL BESTSELLING AUTHOR

"As engaging as the debut, this exciting blend of police procedural and legal thriller recalls the early works of Scott Turow and Lisa Scottoline."
LIBRARY JOURNAL

"The well-crafted storyline makes this a worthwhile

read. Stuffed with gratuitous sex and over-the-top violence, this novel has a riveting plot."
Kirkus Reviews

"Verdict: The pacing is relentless in this debut, a hard-boiled novel with a shocking ending. The supershort chapters will please those who enjoy a James Patterson–style page-turner"
Library Journal

A "clever and engrossing mystery tale involving gorgeous women, lustful men and scintillating suspense."
ForeWord Magazine

"Part of what makes this thriller thrilling is that you sense there to be connections among all the various subplots; the anticipation of their coming together keeps the pages turning."
Booklist

"This is one of the best thrillers I've read yet."
New Mystery Reader Magazine

"A superb thriller and an exceptional read."
Midwest Book Review

"Verdict: This fast-paced book offers fans of commercial thrillers a twisty, action-packed thrill

ride."
Library Journal

"Another masterpiece of action and suspense."
New Mystery Reader Magazine

"Fast paced and well plotted . . . While comparisons will be made with Turow, Grisham and Connelly, Jagger is a new voice on the legal/thriller scene. I recommend you check out this debut book, but be warned . . . you are not going to be able to put it down."
Crimespree Magazine

"A chilling story well told. The pace never slows in this noir thriller, taking readers on a stark trail of fear."
Carolyn G. Hart, N.Y. Times and USA Today Bestselling Author

SHORT
CUTS

R.J. JAGGER

Thriller Publishing Group, Inc.

SHORT CUTS

Thriller Publishing Group, Inc.
Golden, Colorado 80401

Copyright©RJJagger

Library of Congress Control Number: Available

ISBN 978-1-937888-64-0

For Eileen

Table of Contents

ATTORNEY PREY

R.J. JAGGER

DAY ONE

July 26
Wednesday

1

Wednesday night after dark Nick Teffinger sat in the garage behind the wheel of his '67 Corvette and watched a mean thunderstorm pound Denver. The top was down and the seat was pushed back to give his 34-year-old, six-two frame room to breathe. He had two Bud Lights in his gut and a third in his hand. Lightning shredded the sky again and again and filled the universe with a rolling sea of drums.

The wind shook the trees with a demonic possession.

His house was near the top of Green Mountain, fifteen miles west of downtown, on a dead-end street. Traffic was minimal even in good weather so it was unusual when headlights punched up the asphalt. To Teffinger's surprise they stopped in front of his house and went out. A solitary figure emerged and splashed through puddles up the driveway, hunched against the storm.

It was a female figure with a posture he didn't recognize.

The woman walked into the garage, briefly stared at the windshield as if to verify someone was behind it, then opened the passenger door and slipped in.

"You don't know me," she said. "My name's Tangiers Vendora."

Her voice was a song.

The light wasn't much but was enough for Teffinger to see a riveting beauty with blond hair and a fit body in a short white sundress. The woman grabbed his hand and placed it on her chest.

"Do you feel my heart beating?" she said.

He did.

"It's a madman and I'll tell you why. At midnight, someone's going to die. It's either going to be me, or you, or a man named John."

Teffinger pulled his hand away and took a long swallow from the blue can.

"This is a joke, right? Sydney? Is that who put you up to this?"

"This isn't a joke," she said. "This is the furthest thing from a joke you'll ever find."

The words were laced with stress.

They made no sense but Teffinger found no lies.

"Tell me what's going on," he said.

"It's a long story," she said. "It relates to Brittany Asher."

The name sent bark and bite into Teffinger's brain.

Brittany Asher, a pretty little waitress at the time, was one of the sickest murders Teffinger had ever come across. It happened eleven months ago on a warm August night on the east side of Denver in a frugal but relatively stable neighborhood. The killer had a neat way of doing it. He broke in sometime around midnight while the woman was deep in sleep in her own bed. He held a chemical-soaked cloth over her mouth until she passed out. While she was unconscious, he tied her spread-eagle to the bed with 3/8" blue rope. When she started to regain consciousness, the fun part started. He inserted a metal device into her mouth that kept it locked in an open position. He didn't rape her or lick her tits or stomach. The best guess, though, was that he taunted her with what he was about to do.

Then he did it.

"It" was to drop a baby rattlesnake, not more than three inches long, into her mouth then close it off with duct tape. Baby rattlers, Teffinger later learned, have the same venom as the adults and are just as deadly, in fact even more so because they can't control the amount of venom they inject and have a tendency to overkill.

The bite of the fangs eventually occurred, possibly after a period of time, possibly in response to a moving tongue that could no longer be kept still, and possibly immediately. There was no concrete evidence one way or the other as to the quickness with which the bite occurred.

What was certain was that it always occurred, and in Brittany Asher's case, several times over.

The tongue and the inside of her mouth swelled.

That restricted the air and resulted in suffocation.

When the killer left, he made no effort to hide the method of murder. The mouth device was abandoned in place. The snake was also left in place. By the time the crime was discovered, the snake was dead. An autopsy was never performed on it but the best guess was that it either suffocated to death or got constricted and squashed by the very swelling it created.

That's how Brittany Asher died in August of last year.

She wasn't the first to meet that fate, however.

It turned out she was the third.

Six months before her, in February of last year, there was Jacqueline Squares, a New Jersey schoolteacher, killed in the exact same manner, right down to the blue rope, the identical-matching mouth device and the rattlesnake. She was number two of three.

Five months before her, in September of the year before last, a Miami model by the name of Lori Rain died the exact same way. She was number one of three.

The victims had three things in common.

They were all in their mid to late twenties, they all lived alone, and they were all attractive.

Those were old memories.

Now, tonight, a woman named Tangiers Vendora was sitting in Teffinger's car to talk to him about something that related to Brittany Asher.

Her face was intense.

Her skirt had ridden up almost to her panties.

Strong shapely legs, slightly spread, stuck out.

Teffinger took a swallow of beer and said, "What's your interest in Brittany Asher?"

The woman put her hand on his knee.

"Before we go any further, I have to have your 100 percent promise that everything I tell you will remain absolutely confidential. You need to promise that you'll never tell anybody what I'm about to tell you."

"Why?"

"Just promise."

Teffinger frowned.

"I can't promise that if I don't know what you're going to say."

"Just do it," she said. "We don't have time to

play games."

He exhaled.

There was something in her voice that wouldn't be denied.

"Okay," he said. "You have my word."

"Good," she said. "Before I tell you what I'm going to tell you, though, I need to know one thing, and I want you to be absolutely honest with me. How did it feel when you murdered Peyton Rekker?"

2

How did it feel when you murdered Pey-ton Rekker?" That was the question that came from the lips of this mysterious woman sitting next to Teffinger.

"I didn't murder Peyton Rekker," he said.

The woman ran her fingers through Teffinger's hair.

"Okay, let me rephrase it," she said. "How did it feel when you killed him?"

Lightning arced across the sky followed by a slap of thunder.

"It felt like he was resisting arrest."

"Peyton Rekker didn't murder Brittany Asher," the woman said.

Teffinger swallowed what was left of the beer, crushed the can in his fist and threw it into the storm.

"That's bullshit," he said.

"Unfortunately it's not. Tell me something, how

did you find out about him to begin with? I'll bet everything I own that someone made an anonymous call to you. Am I right?"

She was right.

Teffinger's mouth didn't admit it though.

"Why should I talk to you about any of this?"

"Because I have answers you're going to want to hear," she said. "Like I said, Peyton Rekker didn't murder Brittany Asher. You killed the wrong man."

Teffinger slammed his hand on the dash.

"Rekker killed Brittany and I killed him. Since that day not one other person has been killed the way she was. That in and of itself proves that Rekker was the killer."

He opened the car door.

"Where you going?"

"To get another beer. Do you want one?"

She grabbed his arm and pulled him back.

"No and neither do you," she said. "I need you sober. In roughly two hours someone is going to die. I don't want it to be you or me."

Teffinger broke loose, stood up and shut the door.

Then he leaned in and said, "Look, lady, you're pretty, I'll give you that. But as far as making sense goes, you're not doing it. I don't know what your interest is in all this but you're prying into things that are dead and finished."

He left.

Inside, he grabbed two beers, popped one and drank a third of it in one long swallow. For a heartbeat he contemplated going to bed. Instead he headed back to the car, handed a beer to Tangiers and said, "If you think you can make sense, do it. I have to warn you though I'm losing patience."

She eyed the beer in her hand as if it was the enemy, then opened it up and took a swallow.

"Peyton Rekker was framed," she said. "The person who killed Brittany Asher is still out there and I know who he is."

Teffinger cocked his head.

"Okay, who is he?"

"His name's John."

"John?"

"Right, John. He's going to strike again tonight at midnight."

Teffinger shook his head in disbelief.

"And how would you know this?"

She took a sip of beer.

"Because I'm his lawyer," she said. "I'm going to fill you in but first get back to my question. Did you get onto Rekker from an anonymous call?"

Teffinger reflected back.

"That's right."

"That's what I thought," Tangiers said. "Tell me as clearly as you can remember exactly what the caller said."

"Why?"

"Just indulge me, please."

Teffinger considered it.

He saw no downside.

"He said he was a lawyer. He didn't give me his name but he made it clear that the conversation needed to be off the record. He said he could get disbarred if it ever got out what he was doing. He was going to violate the attorney-client privilege and tell me things about one of his clients, things that had been communicated to him in trust. I agreed that I'd keep it all on the hush-hush."

Tangiers made a noise.

"What's wrong?"

"I'll tell you in a minute," she said. "Keep talking."

Teffinger took a swallow of beer.

"Well, he told me that his client was a man named Peyton Rekker. He said that Rekker had confessed to him that he killed three women, one named Lori Rain in Miami, one named Jacqueline Squares in New Jersey and a third named Brittany Asher in Denver."

"When did the call come?"

"What do you mean?"

"In relation to Brittany Asher's murder," she said. "Was it the next day? A week later, or what?"

"I'd say that's about right," Teffinger said. "A week later, give or take. Anyway, I now had the killer's name but I had no source that I could cite. There was no way to get a search warrant. I don't ordinarily do this, but I was so upset about the way Brittany was killed that I decided to pay a little visit to Rekker's house, off the record."

"You mean illegally."

"Right, I broke in," Teffinger said. "Then I found stuff."

"What kind of stuff?"

"Good stuff. The guy had a garage and one of the walls had a number of cabinets, almost like the kind you'd find in a kitchen, with doors on them. They were cheap pine, painted white. In one of those cabinets on a top shelf was a box. Inside that box I found a couple hundred feet of 3/8" blue rope, plus three metal devices that exactly matched what we found in Brittany's mouth. Next to that box was another box. Inside that box was a small glass aquarium, maybe two or three gallons in size, with a tightly weaved mesh wire top covering it. Inside that aquarium were four baby rattlesnakes, the exact size and coloring of the one that was put into Brittany Asher's mouth."

"So what'd you do?"

"I put everything back exactly as I found it and got out of there without anyone seeing me," Teffinger said. "I was illegal at that point, illegal as hell. I couldn't tell anyone in the department what I was up to without dragging them into it. So I kept my mouth shut and started following Rekker around on my own, waiting for him to do something that would justify my making contact with him. During that contact I was going to plant a small amount of drugs on him. That would allow me to make an arrest and subsequently get a warrant for his house, ostensibly to look for more drugs. During that drug hunt, the plan was to accidentally find all the murder paraphernalia."

"You were over the line."

He nodded.

"Way over. The case upset me to that extreme. Anyway, I was staked out down the street from his house one night. He appeared from out of the blue, dragged me out of the car and punched me in the face. I had an assault at that point in time, which is exactly what I needed. I identified myself as a detective and told him he was under arrest. He resisted and forced me into a position to defend myself. He ended up dead in the process."

"Silence.

"You choked him to death," Tangiers said.

"It was self defense."

"Was it?"

"Yes," Teffinger said. "There was a full internal investigation. I was cleared."

She nodded.

"I know that," she said. "But just between you and me and the storm, we both know you could have backed off and taken him alive."

Teffinger said nothing.

He took a sip of beer.

Tangiers patted his knee and said, "Your secret's safe with me. In fact, that's the answer I wanted to hear. I wanted to know that you killed him."

"Why?"

"Because I need you to kill him again."

"That doesn't make sense."

"There's anger in your voice," she said. "Keep it there. You're going to need it."

3

This is going to be awkward because when you got that anonymous call before, the guy said he was an attorney," Tangiers said. "He wasn't an attorney. Do you know who he was?"

"I told you, he didn't give me his name."

"He was the man who killed Brittany Asher. He was pretending to be an attorney and the call was made to frame Rekker and get himself off your radar."

Teffinger heard the words.

His brain processed them.

His heart processed them even harder.

"Why would he frame Rekker?"

"I don't know why it was Rekker instead of someone else but I do know it was a frame-up," Tangiers said. "Think about it. What exactly did you find at his house? Two boxes of conveniently placed incriminating stuff, two boxes that were planted there and that he never even knew about."

The words beat inside Teffinger's head with the force of a hammer.

If they were true, he'd killed an innocent man.

"There's no reason to say it was a frame-up instead of exactly what it was," he said.

"Yes there is."

"And what's that?"

"He told me so."

"You're in touch with him?"

She nodded.

"I'm his lawyer."

Teffinger shook his head in disbelief. "Just like the other guy said he was his lawyer."

She exhaled.

"That's the awkward part," she said. "I didn't know he used that line on you." A beat then, "Here's the situation. I'm a lawyer here in Denver in the Grashnee firm over on Welton."

Teffinger nodded.

He knew the outfit.

They did criminal defense work.

"A man named John called the office one day about wanting to possibly retain one of the lawyers in the office and I was the one who ended up doing the intake," she said. "He said he wanted to talk to me about the possible defense of a criminal act but first wanted to be absolutely positive that what he told me would remain in absolute confidence."

"Okay."

"We talked about the attorney-client privilege and how the privilege belonged to the client and not the lawyer. We talked about how attorneys were bound by both the law and the rules of professional conduct to not betray the confidences of their clients and how, if a lawyer did, what they said could never be used as evidence in court, not to mention that they would be disbarred."

The storm howled.

Lightning exploded so close that Teffinger jumped.

"Go on," he said.

"Well, after he got comfortable with the fact that I was duty bound to keep his secrets secret, he told me he was the one who killed Brittany Asher. He said he was telling me now because if he ever got caught, he wanted me to be his lawyer. He wanted me to monitor what the police were doing and to line up every defense possible in advance."

"Did you do that? Monitor what we were doing?"

She nodded.

"He sent us a cash retainer of $10,000 and we opened a file."

"Did you have his name at that point?"

"No, the only name we had was John," she said. "We had an informal meeting with a few of the lawyers in the office and decided that it wouldn't be improper to open a file even if we didn't know the client's full name. Anyway, during a subsequent conversation, one of the things I talked to him about was a defense commonly used by attorneys that the client couldn't be the guilty one if someone else committed the crime," she said. "In hindsight, now that I think about it, that conversation took place three days or four days after Brittany Asher was murdered, which would have been before he called you. In fact, that's probably how he came up with the idea to pretend he was a lawyer."

Teffinger swallowed.

The story was making more and more sense.

The specter that he had killed an innocent man was correspondingly become more and more real.

"The next time we talked was several days later," she said. "During that conversation, he told me that he took my words to heart and decided to make it look like someone else committed the crime. He told me he planted incriminating evidence in the garage of a man named Peyton Rekker and then made an anonymous call to the detective in charge to the effect that Rekker was the killer."

"Meaning me," Teffinger said.

She nodded.

"Right, you." She took a sip of beer and added, "Then a few days later the news hit that the prime suspect in Brittany Asher's murder had died in a police confrontation while resisting arrest. I dug deeper and found that you actually choked him to death during a struggle."

Teffinger frowned.

"I didn't choke him to death," he said. "My thumbs collapsed his windpipe and that's how he suffocated, not from prolonged pressure."

"Like I said before, your secret's safe with me," she said. "Anyway, the news got out that the police made a conclusive determination that Rekker was the killer and then closed the case."

Teffinger nodded.

That was true.

"John sort of dropped out of sight at that point," Tangiers said. "He stopped calling."

"Your job was done."

"True," she said. "There was a problem though. I kept picturing him dropping that rattlesnake into Brittany's mouth. It was so bizarre that I couldn't get it out of my head. I started waking up in the middle of the night thinking about it. I tried to shrug it off as baggage that comes with being a defense attorney, but it was hard. Then one day in March of this year, the second week of March to be exact, I got a call from John. He said he might need my services in the future."

"He killed someone else?"

"Exactly," she said. "But he had morphed by that time. All the media attention he got from his three rattlesnake victims was exhilarating but in the end it scared the shit out of him and wore him down. He dropped that entire way of murder. His new routine was to abduct the woman, take her to a pre-arranged secluded place and have his fun. Afterwards, he buried her. All the police ended up with was a missing-woman case."

"So who did he kill in March?"

"He wouldn't say," she said. "He wasn't giving me the same amount of details as he was before. It wasn't someone from Denver though. The only thing he told me is that it was someone from Illinois."

"Chicago."

"Maybe. For me, the nightmares started coming back. Then one night I knew what I needed to do. I needed to find out who he was. Without the firm knowing anything about it, I hired a private investigator by the name of Charlene Banta, who has an office over on Market Street. Do you know her?"

No, he didn't.

"I hired her on my own dime and warned her up front that the case could be very, very dangerous," she said. "She took the case anyway. It took until last month, June, three months from when she started, but she finally tracked him down. He has a house near Wash Park. She broke into it and found two things of relevance. The first was a set of files filled with newspaper articles and web printouts regarding the murders of Lori Rain, Jacqueline Squares, Brittany Asher and Trisha Williams."

"Who's Trisha Williams?"

"She's a woman who disappeared in Chicago in March and has never been heard from since."

"So she's the one he called you about," Teffinger said.

"That's my guess," she said. "The investigator, Charlene Banta, also found one other thing of interest. The man had three of those little black mileage calendars, one for this year and two others for the preceding two years. In those calendars were the names of the four women he murdered. Their names were hand-written on the dates he killed them, together with their cities. Each entry had two red circles around it. There was nothing written in any of the books other than those entries. It was a murder log in effect."

Teffinger looked at his watch.

It was 10:30.

In an hour and a half it would be midnight.

"Keep talking," he said.

"I am. Anyway, there was one other entry," she said. "It was for midnight tonight. The two red circles were there and inside was a woman's name."

"What'd it say?"

"It said Tangiers Vendora, Denver, Colorado."

"That's you," Teffinger said.

"Right, I know."

"So he's going to kill you at midnight."

"That's his plan." She put her hand on his arm. "Our plan is different though. Our plan is that we're going to kill him when he comes to kill me."

4

Tangiers' plan to kill John when he came to kill her didn't sit well with Teffinger. He wasn't a killer; he was the opposite. Plus he'd already killed Rekker who, in hindsight, was an innocent man. Sure, Teffinger had been fighting for his life and legally speaking the act was one of self-defense, but deep down in his bones when no one was looking he had to confess that there might have been a little more strangulation involved than what he'd portrayed. The man's windpipe had collapsed, that was true, but maybe not right away.

"No killing," he said. "We'll take him down but it's going to be by the books."

"It can't be by the books."

"Why not?"

"There are no books left."

Teffinger scrunched his face.

"What does that mean?"

"It means this," Tangiers said. "I wanted to see

the files and the mileage calendars for myself so Charlene Banta broke in again and this time I went with her. Everything was gone. The files were gone, the calendars were gone, and as far as we could tell, every shred of evidence that he even lifted a finger was gone. He'd totally cleaned the place up."

Teffinger tilted his head.

"We can still get him."

"How?" Tangiers said. "First of all, everything that I've told you is off the books, and even if we agreed to put it on the books, meaning I would get disbarred, it would be inadmissible in court. It's not evidence in any way shape or form. Second of all, any evidence that might have existed at his home is gone. When you add the two together, what you have is no evidence at all."

Teffinger considered it.

"There could be trace evidence," he said. "Fibers or hairs or something like that."

"That's a long shot," she said. "Even if we went that route, this whole conversation between you me, plus the illegal break in by Charlene Banta, all of that would have to come out, unless you're prepared to sit around and lie about it time after time. He'd find out how I betrayed him. He'd find a way to get me. If he couldn't do it himself he'd hire someone to do it." A beat then, "Even if something matched up, it would be circumstantial. What we need to do is let him come for me. I'll be the bait. When he breaks in, that will be an illegal act. You can be there and will be justified in stopping him."

"That doesn't mean I can kill him."

"No, not if he just holds his hands up and surrenders," she said. "That's not going to happen though. He's going to resist. He's going to attack. You'll be in the exact same position you were with Rekker. This is your chance to kill the right man. It will be fast and clean. Everything will be over and done with. "

Teffinger pictured it.

To his surprise, the picture wasn't distasteful.

If the man forced Teffinger into a life or death battle, well, that would be that. One of them would live and one of them would die.

"Teffinger, there's something I have to tell you," Tangiers said. "He's big. He's bigger than you by at least an inch. He's six-three and maybe six-four."

"What's his physique?"

"He's a gorilla," she said. "You can't let it turn into a fistfight. You need to shoot him. If he gets the edge on you he'll kill you and then he'll kill me."

He considered it.

Shooting would be justified if the man was charging.

The bullet needed to go into his chest or face, not his back.

"Okay," he said.

"Okay what?"

"Okay, I'm in. We'll set up at your place and let him make his move. If he forces us into a situation where he needs to die, then that's what happens. It'll be for Brittany."

Tangiers clinked her beer can against his.

"For Brittany," she said.

"What's this guy's last name, by the way?"

"I'll tell you after."

"Why not now?"

"I don't want you to change your mind and start thinking about a search warrant," she said. "Don't let me die tonight, Teffinger. That's all I ask."

"I won't."

"Promise me."

He put his arm around her shoulders.

"That's not the kind of thing I can promise and you know it," he said.

"I don't care. Just say the words."

He squeezed her.

"Okay, I promise."

5

Tangiers lived in a standalone Tudor on the east edge of Denver near Colorado Boulevard where the yards were big and the pockets were deep. Teffinger pulled the Tundra up the woman's cobblestone driveway at 11:03, kissed her deeply as if ending a date, then pulled away and let the taillights get swallowed up by the storm.

Two blocks later he turned a corner, edged to the curb and killed the lights.

His heart raced.

Gorilla.

He couldn't get the word out of his brain.

He checked his weapon, found everything in order and stepped out into the storm. It hadn't let up, not a bit, and if anything was even more wicked. He covered his face as best he could and muscled his body against the weather down a residential street that ran parallel to Tangiers'. Duran Duran's "Rio" ran through his head. He cut through backyards, scaled a wrought-iron fence at the rear of Tangiers' property, and made his way through squishy grass to the back door.

It was locked, as it should be.

He knocked.

Her name is Rio and she dances on the sand ...

A heartbeat later the door opened and Tangiers' face appeared. She pulled Teffinger in, closed the door and locked it. "It's ten after," she said. "We have fifty minutes."

This level of the house was dark.

They headed through that darkness and up a winding staircase to the second story. The master bedroom was large and opulent. The window coverings were open and the storm rattled the glass. Light came from a table lamp in the corner, nothing too bright, from a 60-watt bulb or something to that effect. Tangiers flipped a switch and brought the room into darkness. Teffinger slipped under the bed and said, "Okay."

The light went back on.

"Follow your normal routine," he said. "He's probably watched you a hundred times."

"I know."

That was true, she did know.

That's all they did on the way over; discuss the plan.

Just like that river twisting through a dusty land.

Lightning shot through Teffinger's blood.

If the man actually came—and there was no reason to think he wouldn't—someone would be dead within the hour. It would either be him or Tangiers or John, just like Tangiers said at the beginning. The statement had been so crazy when she said it. Now here it was, as real as real gets.

"I always take a shower before I go to bed," Tangiers said.

"Then take one."

At the end of the bed the woman's dress dropped to the floor, followed by a bra and panties. Then her body came into sight as she walked across the room to the master bathroom.

Her ass was taut.

Her back was strong.

Her legs were perfect.

She flipped the bathroom lights on, dimmed them to half and got the shower up to temperature. Then she stepped in and lathered up.

The shower door was clear glass.

The spray washed against it and brought the woman's body in and out of focus with all the magic of an oasis in the desert.

And when she shines she really shows you all she can.

The bed was closing in on him. Teffinger brought his head and shoulders and arms out from under it, still out of line of sight from a window, and focused on Tangiers.

He couldn't let her die.

She was too beautiful.

She was filled with too much light.

He pulled his weapon out of the holster, flicked the safety off and felt the hardness of the cold steel before placing it on the carpet next to him.

Tangiers had her head under the spray.

Her eyes were closed.

Water cascaded down her face and dripped off her chin and onto her breasts and down her stomach.

Oh Rio, Rio dance across the Rio Grande.

Suddenly a vibration came from somewhere, something that was probably the storm but might not be. Out of an abundance of caution Teffinger turned towards it. His peripheral vision detected a shape swinging savagely from above.

Before he could react his head exploded in pain.

6

Iron fists yanked Teffinger out from under the bed by the hair and then a solid kick smashed into his ribs. The man towering above him had a chiseled face filled with rage. His arms were pythons. Teffinger looked for the gun, saw it to the side and went to grab it. Just as his hand felt the steel a kick from the man's boot sent the weapon flying across the floor. Teffinger grabbed the man's foot and twisted, then got to his feet before the man could stop him.

Blood ran down his forehead and into his eyes.

He wiped it off with the back of his hand and squared off, blinking wildly to get the last drops out.

The man paused and let a smirk creep onto his mouth.

"This is going to be fun," he said.

Then he sprang.

Teffinger was going to die, he knew that, but

he was going to get his licks in before he did. He swung wildly at the man's face with a deathblow and missed. The momentum sent him off balance and tumbling to the floor. Before he could react, the man was on him, pounding his head and neck with furious fists.

Blow after blow after blow came but none killed him.

Then he was on his feet.

Things were squared again.

He charged.

What happened next were the worst moments of his life. At the end he found himself straddling the man's chest and pounding his face into oblivion.

The man stopped moving.

Teffinger pounded more.

All reactions stopped.

Teffinger got to his feet with his hands clenched and dared the man to move a muscle.

The man didn't move.

He looked dead.

Teffinger nudged him with his foot.

No reaction came.

Teffinger's chest heaved as his lungs fought for air. Second after second after second passed and each one brought Teffinger to the realization that the fight was over. The adrenalin drained from his blood and a deep exhaustion filled his muscles, so absolute that it brought him to his knees.

Suddenly Tangiers was at his side.

She had a lamp in her hands and raised it over her head. Then she swung it down. The corner of the lamp's base smashed into the man's forehead and shattered his skull.

Tangiers' arms trembled and her lips quivered.

The lamp dropped from her hands.

Then she sank to the floor next to Teffinger and collapsed in his lap.

7

Time stood still. The storm beat down, the windows rattled and jagged flashes of lightning ripped the sky. Tangiers stood up. She was still without clothes but her body was dry. She sat on the bed and put her face in her hands. Then she looked at Teffinger and said, "I just killed a man."

"No you didn't, I did."

"We don't know that."

"Yes we do. I could feel the life leaving his body the last time I punched him," Teffinger said. "That's why I stopped. It was over. He was dead."

"He could have just been unconscious."

Teffinger opened his mouth to rebut it.

No words came out.

She was right.

"I could go down for murder," Tangiers said.

"That won't happen."

She stood up and paced. Panic had a solid stranglehold on her face.

"If he died from you, that was self-defense," she said. "But if he died from me, it wasn't. It was murder."

Teffinger exhaled.

Legally speaking, that was true.

The man was unconscious and had been for many seconds at the point in time when Tangiers smashed him. He was no threat to either of them at that point. They were not in a defensive mode. They had been earlier, granted, but they weren't at that point. The act, when reduced to its essence, was one of aggression against an unconscious man. It was understandable and it was no doubt powered in large part by a continuing rush of adrenalin, but it was still unnecessary.

It was excessive.

"So what do you want to do?" Teffinger said.

"I can't go to jail," Tangiers said. "We should just get out of here, both of us, right now."

Teffinger got to his feet, staggered to the bed and collapsed backwards onto the mattress.

"Turn the lights off," he said.

Tangiers did.

The darkness was cool water on Teffinger's brain.

"You might have a point about leaving," he said. "We could wipe the place clean of my fingerprints and then leave. You could come home in an hour or so and find the body. Then you'd call 911."

Tangiers laid down next to Teffinger and draped an arm across his chest.

"You would do that for me?"

He exhaled.

"I'm 99 percent sure that I'm the one who killed him and that we could simply make the 911 call right now and tell the truth," he said. "But I have to admit I'm not a hundred percent sure. There's no use taking a chance on your future."

She kissed him.

"Thank you."

"We're inside the Denver city limits," he said. "When you make the call it's going to end up going to my department. A detective by the name of Sydney Heatherwood is on duty tonight. She'll get the assignment but she'll call me. That's standard practice. I can show up to back her up on the investigation. What I'll do when I get here is forget to put my gloves on. That way if my fingerprints end up getting lifted off something, there'll be an explanation. The secret though is to not let that happen. We need to be really careful and wipe down anything and everything that I might have touched."

He edged up into a sitting position.

"Is that our plan?" he said.

"Yes."

"Okay," he said. "But going forward we need

to be real clear on our story that neither one of us was here. If I end up getting caught in a lie, my career as a detective is over. I might also be facing obstruction of justice charges; you too for that matter. That won't look so hot on your resume."

She frowned.

"Teffinger, I don't know if I can put you in that position. Maybe we should just tell the truth and hope the autopsy comes out the right way."

"Look," he said. "It took a lot of guts for you to play the bait tonight. This asshole would be walking the streets tomorrow if it wasn't for you. So now you get a little respect in return, okay?"

A beat then, "Okay."

"Good. Let's get busy."

DAY TWO

July 27
Thursday

8

Lots of women had paraded in and out of Teffinger's life over the years. Tangiers was the latest to parade in and Teffinger was already to a point where it would hurt if she paraded out. He could see spending time with her, not just for a few sex-infused weeks or months, but well after the initial exhilaration wore off and they were left with their more naked souls.

It was 1:18 a.m. when his home phone rang and Sydney's voice came through. "Got some job security," she said. "A woman came home and found a dead man in her bedroom. I'm on my way over. You want to join me?"

Sure.

Why not?

"Give me the address."

She did.

It was Tangiers' house.

Outside the storm still raged.

He swung by the all-night Conoco on Simms long enough to get a thermos of coffee and mentally retraced the interior of the house as he drove, searching for a place his fingerprints might have been left.

He couldn't find any.

When he got to the scene, several cop cars were parked in the street, busy throwing eerie red and blue jabs of light into the weather.

He checked in with the scribe and headed upstairs, forgetting to put his gloves on.

The dead man was as Teffinger had left him.

He hadn't been moved.

Sydney was at the body studying the wounds. She was 27, athletic and the only female African-American in the department. Technically she was still the newbie although she'd already cut her teeth on Denver's worst. Teffinger personally stole her last year out of the vice department. He handed her a disposable cup and filled it from the thermos.

"What happened to your face?" she asked.

"I had a little incident in a bar. It was sort of a Bad Bad Leroy Brown situation."

"Bad who?"

"Leroy Brown, you know, the Jim Croce song."

"Never heard of it."

"It involves the wife of a jealous man. In my defense, I didn't know she was married. She wasn't wearing a ring. And I wasn't the one who approached her. She approached me." He nodded towards the body. "So what's your theory?"

"My theory is that he's a lot like you. He lost the fight."

Teffinger smiled.

"The fight with who?"

She shrugged.

"I don't know. According to the owner, she came home and voila, there he was. She says she's never seen him before in her life. It's like he just dropped out of the sky and landed here."

"He's not an old boyfriend or anything?"

"Not according to her." She took a sip of coffee and said, "It's possible this was a robbery that started out with two people. They got into an argument for whatever reason smack dab in the middle of it."

Teffinger nodded.

It was possible

"Who's the owner?"

"She's a single female. They got her out in one of the cars."

"I'll be right back."

"Don't hit on her."

He grinned.

"Never."

"She's pretty."

"It doesn't matter."

He headed downstairs, got directed to the car

where the owner was being held and slipped inside.

The person in the back seat was a woman.

She was pretty but she wasn't Tangiers.

"Sorry," Teffinger said. "I was looking for the owner."

"That's me."

The words took him by surprise.

"That's you?"

"Right." She extended her hand. "Jamie Parker."

"Let me see if I have this right," Teffinger said. "You own this house?"

"Correct."

"And do you live in it?"

"Also correct."

"Do you have any roommates?"

"No."

Teffinger's heart raced.

"Do you have any guests staying with you or anything like that?"

"No, I live here by myself," she said. "I was at a club with a girlfriend and when I came home there was a dead man in my bedroom." A beat then, "I don't understand why I have to wait out here in a car."

"It's standard procedure to remove all civilians from the scene," he said. "That keeps it from getting contaminated. It doesn't mean you're in trouble or anything."

"Okay."

"We'll take you downtown and get your statement," he said. "Then you'll be free to go."

"Back home?"

He frowned.

"We'll probably have the place sealed for at least three or four days. Do you have any idea what happened?"

She shook her head.

"Negative," she said. "I came home to a body. That's all I know."

Teffinger said his goodbyes and stepped out into the weather.

Tangiers had lied to him.

It wasn't her house at all.

What the hell was going on?

9

Teffinger worked the crime scene until four in the morning and then left Sydney to wrap up. He was exhausted enough to sleep for two days but Tangiers' lie had his brain on fire. The more he thought about it the more ominous it became. He twitched and turned hour after hour in that nowhere state that wasn't quite sleep and wasn't quite awake, then pulled himself out of bed shortly after eight, showered and hopped in the Tundra, heading east towards Denver on the 6th Avenue freeway.

In his left hand was a cup of coffee.

In his lap was a bowl of cereal.

In his blood was a steady stream of acid.

The fact that Tangiers didn't live in the house like she said she did was only one of two little surprises from last night. The other was that the dead man carried no wallet or identification. As of this point in time he was John Doe. If Teffinger was the one who killed him, he didn't even know the man's name.

It was 9:02 a.m. when Teffinger got to Tangiers' place of employment, namely Grashnee, Dodge & White, P.C. on Welton Street. The office was a renovated two-story wooden structure that had the architecture of the early 1900's. It might have been a private mansion or a store in its past life. Now it was something ancient with fresh paint, awash in a sea of things that were taller and newer.

The walkway from the street to the front door was paved brick.

The door was wooden, heavy and painted a rust color.

Matching awnings hung over all the front-facing windows.

Immediately inside the front door was a reception area.

Behind the reception desk was a mature woman with a nice smile. Behind her was a fern.

Teffinger put on his best smile and said, "I'm here to see Tangiers Vendora."

The woman scrunched her face.

"Who?"

"Tangiers Vendora."

"There's nobody here by that name," she said.

"She's one of your lawyers."

"No, we have no lawyers here by that name."

Teffinger shuffled his feet.

"She's blond, late-twenties and fairly attractive."

The woman frowned.

"I'm sorry but I don't think you're in the right place. The firm only has one female attorney. She has black hair and is in her forties."

He said, "Thanks.'

Then he was gone.

The Colorado sun was bright and snapped into his eyes. Ordinarily it went straight to his brain and made everything right.

This time it didn't.

From the law firm Teffinger headed to Market Street to talk to the private investigator, Charlene Banta, who Tangiers hired to find out who her mystery client "John" was.

The investigator existed but was genuinely confused.

"I've never had a client by the name of Tangiers Vendora."

Teffinger described her appearance.

Banta never had a client by that description.

"Would you tell me if you did?"

"If I did in fact do work for such a person, I might or might not disclose it depending on the nature of the case," she said. "But if I never had such a client, I don't have a problem affirmatively stating that I never had such a client. It's not an ethical breach to admit that you never had a client that you in fact never had. In this case, I'm telling you point blank that I never had a client named Tangiers Vendora, I never had a case for a woman by the physical description that you gave me, and I never had a case for a lawyer trying to find out who her client was."

"Okay, thanks."

"I'm sorry."

If there had been any doubt before there was none now. Tangiers, if in fact that was even her real name, had set him up from the start to kill a man.

He'd fallen prey to her pretty little face and her pretty little white dress so innocently hiked up to her panties. He'd put his hand on her heart. He'd watched the water cascade down her curvy little body in the shower.

Where was she right now at this moment?

Who was the man she got him to kill?

Why did she want him dead?

Suddenly a dark thought twisted into Teffinger's brain.

Maybe she didn't set him up to kill someone after all.

Maybe she set him up to be the one who got killed.

Maybe he was the one who was supposed to die in the fight. Maybe that's why the guy was already in the house and got a jump on him.

Maybe Tangiers was out there right now thinking of a way to finish what she started.

10

At homicide he called the Medical Examiner, Bob Nelson, a man with a perpetual patina of liquor on his breath, to see if he'd had a chance to take a look at the body yet.

He hadn't.

"When you get to it, I'm curious about that blow to the head that smashed the guy's skull in," Teffinger said.

"Curious in what way?"

"I'd like to know if that's the final blow that killed him or whether the guy continued to beat him even after that."

"Well, that much I can already tell you," Nelson said. "That blow was post-mortem. It caused no bleeding."

"So he was already dead, that's what you're saying."

"That's what post-mortem means, Teffinger. He may have gotten beaten more after that, I'll take a look, but he was already dead when that blow came."

"You're sure?"

"Positive."

Teffinger hung up

He was the killer, not Tangiers.

He needed air, not in ten minutes, now, and headed outside to get it, walking briskly into the guts of the city with no destination.

The sun beat down.

Sweat rolled down his face.

Tangiers.

Tangiers.

Tangiers.

Who was she?

Her story was that she was a criminal defense lawyer. It seemed so real when she talked. She knew the language. She knew the system. She knew about privilege and confidentiality. She had the hardness to defend someone she knew was guilty. When Teffinger closed his eyes he could see her standing before a jury.

"Ninety percent," he said to himself.

That's how sure he was that Tangiers really was a lawyer.

In the 1400 block of Larimer Street he spotted a worn bronze sign on the side of an equally worn building that said, Bryson Wilde, Private Investigator, 201.

He headed up a set of rickety wooden steps to the second floor, opened the door to 201 and stepped inside. A man was pacing next to the window with a smoke in one hand and a cup of coffee in the other. He had blond hair, longer than most, combed straight back.

He had the build and swagger of a ladies man.

"Are you Bryson Wilde?"

The man sized him up.

"The third, to be precise. My grandfather opened this place back in '52."

"I want you to find someone for me," Teffinger said.

"Who?"

"A woman. She's about twenty-eight or twenty-nine, five-six and drop-dead gorgeous with a body built for sin."

Wilde smiled.

"I've been looking for the same woman," he said. "If I ever find her I'm keeping her for myself."

Teffinger knew he should smile.

He couldn't.

"I'm about 90% sure she's a criminal defense lawyer," he said. "Her hair's long and blond, but it could have been dyed."

Wilde took a drag on the butt and blew smoke.

"What else you got on her?"

"Nothing."

"Nothing?"

"No, that's it."

"That's a tall drink of water," Wilde said.

"What's your price for drinking these days?"

Wilde frowned.

"It ain't cheap," he said. "A hundred an hour plus expenses."

Teffinger pulled a check out of his wallet, filled it out for $5,000, handed it to the man and said, "Can you get started right away?"

He could.

He could indeed.

Teffinger was almost out the door when the man said, "What city does she live in?"

"Unknown."

Then he was gone.

At street level he heard his name shouted from above. It was Wilde, leaning out the window.

"This is a long shot," Wilde said. "I can't give you any guarantees."

"I understand."

"I know who you are, I've seen you on TV."

"Keep everything confidential."

"That much I can guarantee."

Teffinger headed over to the 16th Street Mall and walked on the shady side. He was ten minutes into it when he turned around and headed back to Wilde's office.

"There's one more piece of information," he said.

Wilde tapped two cigarettes loose from a pack and extended one to Teffinger who declined. Wilde lit his up, blew smoke and said, "No one smokes any more. What's the other piece?"

"Well it's two pieces, actually. First, the woman goes by the name Tangiers Vendora."

"Is that an alias or her real name?"

"I think it's an alias," Teffinger said. "I Googled it ten different ways and it never attached to anything. The second thing is that she's somehow connected to a woman named Jamie Parker who's a lawyer at Roberts & Morrison."

"Connected how?"

"I don't know," Teffinger said. "They might be in some kind of conspiracy together."

"Conspiracy to do what?"

Teffinger shrugged.

Then his face hardened.

"It might be a conspiracy to kill someone."

"Who?"

"Me, possibly."

"You?"

Teffinger nodded.

"Possibly," he said. "That's the key word. It may or may not be the case."

Wilde took a deep drag, looked out the window

and then back at Teffinger.

"If that's true, I'll have to sneak up on her from behind."

"Then do it."

"This case is getting big," Wilde said.

"Do what it takes," Teffinger said. "There's more money if you need it. Just be honest and don't gouge me."

"I won't." A beat then, "You have resources. Why aren't you doing this yourself?"

"Because it's off the record. Be sure it stays that way."

DAY NINE

August 3
Thursday

11

A full week passed and not an iota of progress was made on any front. Tangiers remained invisible. The man Teffinger killed still hadn't been identified. A few suspicious cars came up Teffinger's street in the middle of the night but no one had made a direct attempt on his life. The investigator, Bryson Wilde, called on a Thursday morning and reported in a somber voice that the $5,000 retainer was gone.

He needed more money.

Teffinger chewed on it, deciding, then said, "I'll bring you another check."

"When?"

He checked his watch.

"In about an hour."

"I'll be here."

When Teffinger got there Wilde was pacing in front of the window with a smoke in one hand and a cup of coffee in the other. "I've been concentrating on that lawyer here in town, Jamie Parker. If she has anything in her past that's not supposed to be there, I can't find it. She's as clean as a bottle of mineral water."

Teffinger grunted and set a check on the desk.

Wilde glanced at it, left it where it was and said, "If she and the Tangiers woman were in some kind of conspiracy together, they would have been talking. A lot of that talking would have been by cell. I've spent a lot of time trying to get my hands on her records. It sounds like it should be easy but it's not like the old days. They keep them under seal. You don't even know who in the company has access to them. It's almost impossible to find a palm to grease. In fact it's almost impossible to get a human being to talk to."

Teffinger nodded.

He knew that.

"However, I finally got them," Wilde said. "None of the calls panned out to be to or from anyone of interest." He blew smoke and then opened a file on his computer. "Check out these photos and tell me if any of them are Tangiers."

The first photo on the screen was a blond woman.

It wasn't Tangiers.

"Where'd you dig these up from?"

"What I've been doing is making a list of every criminal defense firm in the country that I can find on the web," he said. "Most of those firms have websites. Most of those websites have bios for their attorneys and most of those bios have a head shot. Every time I come to a hot woman in her late twenties, whether she has blond hair or not, I'm downloading the picture. Like I said in the beginning, this whole thing is going to be a long shot. Go ahead and flip through and see if I got lucky."

Teffinger did.

For 22 pictures there was no luck.

Then there was.

Photo 23 was Tangiers.

"I can't believe it."

"That's her?"

"Yes, absolutely."

"Hold on." Wilde cross-referenced to a spreadsheet, then pulled up a website for a firm in San Francisco by the name of Steele & Panders, P.C. On the left was a list of lawyers. He clicked on Tianca Vaughn. Tangiers' face popped up surrounded by a short biography, areas of expertise and links to cases where she had been the attorney of record.

"So her real name's Tianca Vaughn," Teffinger said.

"If that's her, then yes."

"That's her all right."

Wilde lit a cigarette, focused on the check for a moment and said, "I've already gone past the first five you gave me, by three or four or five hundred."

Teffinger left the check where it was.

"Figure out the final bill and mail me whatever you didn't use."

Wilde smiled.

That was good.

"Remember, this whole thing is off the books," Teffinger said.

"I understand."

"I don't mean a little off the books, I mean way off the books."

"As far as I'm concerned, you don't even exit."

Teffinger was almost out the door when he turned and said, "Do me a favor. Find out what you can on Tianca Vaughn. I'll call you tonight some-time tonight."

Wilde blew smoke and said, "Done."

Teffinger's instinct was to dial the woman up and say, "Hi there. Remember me?"

He didn't though.

Instead he drove to DIA and boarded the first plane to San Francisco.

Touchdown at San Francisco International came just as the lights of the city began to twinkle. He rented a black Camry and checked into the Ho-tel California, a few blocks out of the center of the financial district.

He called Wilde and learned that the man hadn't been able to find out much of interest on Tangiers other than she had a solid reputation as one of the better defense attorneys in the city.

Then Teffinger went to bed.

He needed rest.

Tomorrow would be a day that would change his life.

DAY TEN

August 4
Friday

12

Friday morning at seven, Teffinger headed into the guts of the financial district and got himself situated in a Starbucks on Market Street. Across the way on the other side of the trolley line was a contemporary seven-story office building. Inside that building, on the fifth floor, were the offices of Tangiers' firm, Steele & Panders.

Tangiers came into view reporting for work shortly before eight.

The crowd was thick and the time was short but Teffinger fully recognized her. She was wearing two-inch heels, nylons and a gray skirt with a matching jacket. An expensive leather briefcase swung in her right hand. Her face was the face of a lawyer bracing for a long workday.

Teffinger finished his drink and then wandered the city until the noon hour, when Tangiers reappeared. He followed her to a seafood restaurant where she dined with a man who looked like a law-yer. The meal was hurried, no more than 25 min-utes, after which the woman hoofed it back to her office.

The sway in her step was hypnotic.

When Teffinger focused on the movement he could feel his hand on her heart and could hear the shower spray against her body.

She lived in a contemporary ranch in an exclusive neighborhood five miles up 101 on the other side of the Golden Gate Bridge.

Friday afternoon Teffinger parked near a Eu-calyptus grove down the winding lane and head-ed towards the structure on foot, to all intents and purposes just a guy out for a stroll.

The air was a lot cooler than Denver.

A light wind blew.

It was filled with salt.

The property had a four-foot wall in the front near the road, made of stone and covered with growth. A circular cobblestone driveway entered the property at one side, swept past the front door, and exited at the other side. It also branched over to the garage.

Teffinger headed up the cobblestone.

The front door was oversized, contemporary and made of some type of ornate carved wood that Teffinger wasn't familiar with. A narrow curtain window to the side offered a good view into an expansive living space with high ceilings, rich textures and colorful handpicked sittings.

He tried the knob.

It was locked.

He headed around to the back, which turned out to be a wall of windows looking over a redwood deck into the horizon line. The woman's backyard was the ocean. The crashing of the breakers against the crags and cliffs was her music.

The kitchen had a glass door that opened onto the deck.

Right now it was locked.

The master bedroom had a similar door.

It was also locked.

Wooden stairs led from the backyard down to a small beach nested in jagged rocks. Teffinger found a place in the shade and watched the breakers.

Tonight he'd make an unannounced visit to Tangiers.

He'd break through one of the doors if he had to.

He'd find out once and for all what she was up to.

13

Friday night after dark Teffinger parked at the Eucalyptus grove and approached Tangiers' house with a beating heart. A heavy fog raked through the night on a stiff breeze. The woman's white BMW was parked on the cobblestone in front of the entry. No other vehicles were around. The interior lights were on, not more than a watercolor mist from this distance.

He took one step after another after another until he came to the entry.

There he peered through the curtain window.

Several light fixtures were on.

A large flat-panel TV was also on.

The screen showed a Frasier rerun.

In front of the TV was a red leather couch.

No one was on that couch.

Next to the couch was an end table.

On that table was a glass of red wine—one glass of wine, not two as if one for her and one for someone else, only one. It was half full.

Frasier and Niles were arguing about something on the screen.

Nothing in the house moved.

Tangiers might be in the bathroom or the kitchen.

That was fine.

Teffinger could wait.

He had nothing but time.

He waited.

Tangiers didn't appear.

Maybe she got sidetracked in another room by a phone call or an email.

A minute passed and then another.

Teffinger found his feet shifting impatiently.

Then he got a bad feeling in his gut, a feeling that made him look up to see if there was a security camera above the door.

There was.

It was small and hidden but it was definitely there.

Suddenly a noise came from behind him.

He turned just in time to see the shape of a large dark silhouette swinging something at him. He reacted but not fast enough. Something heavy and metal took a solid blow to his shoulder. It knocked him back but not down.

He swung a fist and got face.

Then he swung again and again and again.

The man tried to get away but Teffinger wrestled him to the ground and pounded his face again and again. Then the man landed a blow to Teffinger's face.

His mind snapped.

His thumbs went to the man's throat.

He squeezed.

The man flailed under him but couldn't break his balance. Then the flailing got less and less and finally stopped.

Teffinger got up and hovered over the shape.

It didn't move.

It didn't move an inch.

It looked dead.

He tried the door handle and found it locked.

At his feet was a fireplace iron.

He smashed the curtain window, reached through and unlocked the door.

Then he stepped inside.

"Tangiers!"

No one answer.

"Tangiers!"

Not a sound came from anywhere.

He headed into the guts of the structure one step at a time.

14

He found her in the bedroom tied spread-eagle on the bed with blue rope. Her jaws were jammed open and tape covered her lips. Her eyes were wild with panic and her arms twitched.

"Don't move," he said.

Slowly and carefully he pulled the tape off her mouth a quarter of an inch at a time. The woman's tongue was at the back of her mouth protecting her throat. On that tongue was a small rattlesnake in a calm, laying position.

Teffinger shifted his head to get a better view.

Suddenly the snake curled up and bobbed its head.

"It's okay," Teffinger said. "I'm not going to hurt you."

The bobbing grew more and more agitated.

Then a rattling noise came.

"Calm down," Teffinger said.

The rattling grew louder.

Tears rolled out of Tangiers' eyes but she held every muscle in her body as still as death.

Teffinger put his left hand to the side of the woman's face in a position as if to slap her. Then he pointed his right index finger at the snake from directly above.

It was six inches up.

"Go on, bite this," he said.

The snake bobbed.

Teffinger lowered his finger a half-inch at a time, getting closer and closer.

Suddenly the snake sprang.

Its reach wasn't enough.

The fangs snapped an inch short.

"Good boy," Teffinger said. "One more time."

He got his finger back into position and slowly lowered it.

The snake sprang.

When it did Teffinger slapped at it with his left hand and made contact. Half of the reptile came out of Tangiers' mouth but not all of it.

No one moved.

Tangiers didn't move.

Teffinger didn't move.

The snake didn't move.

A second passed and then another and another.

Then the snake slipped all the way out of the woman's mouth, down the side of her face and away from her head. Teffinger let it be until it got to the edge of the bed and then swatted it off with the back of his hand.

DAY THIRTEEN

August 7
Monday

15

Monday morning Teffinger woke to find the first rays of dawn working their way around the edges of the window coverings and washing the room in a soft ochre patina. Next to him, Tangiers was asleep and breathing deeply, with the lower half of her body covered by a thin sheet. Teffinger studied the curves of her body as he headed for the bathroom and felt sorry for every guy in the world who wasn't him.

He got the shower up to temperature and stepped in.

Everything Tangiers had told him back in that stormy night in the Corvette was true, with a few little twists. She really was a criminal defense lawyer, except it was in San Francisco instead of Denver. She really did have a client named John—John Smith to be precise—who told her that he was the one who killed Brittany Asher and the others before her. He told her he'd set up Peyton Rekker.

It was all in Tangiers' notes. She really did hire a private investigator to track down her client, except it wasn't Charlene Banta in Denver, it was a woman named Patricia Williams in San Francisco.

Those were the little twists.

There was also a big one.

The name of the next victim on John Smith's calendar wasn't Tangiers, it was a woman named Jamie Parker in Denver, Colorado. Tangiers came to town and warned the woman what was going on. She also told her that she had a plan to kill him. All that the woman needed to do was be out of the house that night and then return home and find a dead man in her bedroom.

To make the story stick that she lived in the house that actually belonged to Jamie Parker, she had to change everything about her life to Denver instead of San Francisco.

In hindsight, Tangiers took all the risk herself when she didn't need to.

The man that Teffinger ended up killing that night was in fact the same man who killed Brittany Asher.

As to the attack on Tangiers three days ago, the man didn't die at Teffinger's hands and as of this date no one knew who he was. Their best guess was that he wanted Tangiers dead for some reason and knew about her relationship with John Smith.

Alternatively, someone else wanted Tangiers dead and hired the man.

Either way it was a copycat murder to set Tangiers' client up as the killer. He didn't know that Smith had already been killed.

Why he wanted Tangiers dead was unknown at this point. The plan was for Tangiers to stay in Denver with Teffinger until that part of the puzzle got figured out.

The shower curtain pulled back and Tangiers stepped in.

She slapped Teffinger's ass and said, "You were pretty rough last night."

He kissed her.

"Sorry."

"Don't apologize, it wasn't a complaint." She rubbed her chest on his and said, "By the way, I don't know if I told you this before but the head of the San Francisco homicide unit is on his way out and the position's going to open up. Maybe you should apply for it."

Teffinger cocked his head.

"Maybe I will."

CONFIDENTIAL PREY

R.J. JAGGER

TWO WEEKS BEFORE
IT ALL STARTED

1

A wicked storm fell out of an evil night sky. Nick Teffinger, the 34-year-old head of Denver's homicide unit, was in the thick of it with the Tundra's wipers swishing back and forth to a demonic beat. From the radio Mick was screaming that he couldn't get no satisfaction and Teffinger was screaming right along with him.

'Cause I've tried and I've tried and I've tried and I've tried …

Traffic was minimal.

A woman appeared up ahead at the side of the road, hunched against the weather. Her thumb came out; she was trying to get a ride. Teffinger edged over and powered down the passenger window.

The woman was in her early thirties with dark exotic features. Heavy drenched clothes clung to her body.

Her chest was ample.

She wore no bra.

Her face was serious.

Teffinger unlocked the door and said, "Get in."

She did.

"Thanks, mister."

Her voice was timid and laced with stress.

"Where you going?"

"I don't know."

"Do you need a ride home?"

"Sure if you're going to Seattle."

Her name was Atasha and her story was simple. She and her boyfriend were passing through Colorado on their way from New York to Seattle. Two hours ago they had a fight, not one of those normal ones, a mean one where things got said. He dragged her out of the car and told her to have nice life. Then he was gone. To his credit, it wasn't raining that badly out at the time.

Now it was.

She had less than $30 in her purse.

She had no cell phone.

She was a stray cat out in a stray night.

"I'll get you a hotel room," Teffinger said. "My treat. Then we can touch base in the morning and figure out how to get you back home."

"Thanks but I don't take charity."

"It's not charity. It's just one person helping another."

"I can't take money."

"You can pay it back later if that makes you feel better."

"I don't like owing people either," she said. "Just drop me off anywhere I can get out of the weather. I'll take it from there."

Teffinger argued.

He lost.

He did, however, talk her into at least sleeping on his couch.

His neighborhood was in total darkness when they got there. Not a streetlight was on and not a single light came from inside a house. The storm had defaulted the neighborhood back to its prehistoric days.

Inside, Teffinger got a flashlight for the woman, gave her the best dry clothes he scrounge up—a T, a fresh pair of boxer shorts and white cotton gym socks—and showed her where to dry off.

"I'll be in the garage," he said. "You want some wine or a beer?"

She did.

A beer.

In fact, a beer would be perfect.

"No problem," he said. "Whatever you do, don't look under my mattress."

"Why, what's under your mattress?"

"Nothing. Just don't look there, okay?"

He had the garage door open and his six-two frame was behind the wheel of the '67 Corvette, watching the lightning show, when she showed up. She slid into the passenger seat and flicked the flashlight off.

He popped the top of a blue can and passed it to her.

"This is better than TV," she said.

"Way better." The pounding of the water was so powerful on the ground that it resonated into the garage and up the tires. "Tomorrow morning I'm going to drive you to the airport and get you on a plane back home."

"I told you—"

"I know," he said. "No charity and all that. The problem is there's no way to solve this without getting money involved. I'm not just going to let you wander out into the world with thirty dollars in your pocket."

She took a long swallow.

"We'll see."

He clinked his can on hers.

They talked.

She was sophisticated, educated and, most surprisingly, an ex-marine with two years of her tenure in the Middle East.

"I don't get it," Teffinger said. "How does someone like you end up in a storm with only thirty dollars?"

"It's a long story," she said.

He shrugged.

"I have time."

"It also a private story."

"I won't tell anyone."

"You know what I mean."

He did.

He did indeed.

"So at least we're agreed on the airport tomorrow?" he said.

"Only if I can pay you back."

"You can."

"I'll make you breakfast in the morning," she said. "What do you like?"

He swallowed what was left in the can.

"If you feel like working up some pancakes, I have fresh strawberries and whipped cream."

She shook his hand.

"Deal." A beat then, "I think I'm ready for that couch now."

He checked his watch.

It was 11:02.

It took a solid argument but Teffinger convinced her to take the bed and let him take the couch. He got his frame as comfortable as he could on the cushions, sunk his head into the pillow and closed his eyes.

The intensity of the storm hadn't let up.

The walls creaked and the fireplace whistled.

It was music.

He was almost asleep when he sensed a presence in the room. Then a warm naked body was snuggling up next to him.

Atasha's voice whispered in his ear, "Hi there."

Teffinger's instinct was to screw her so hard there'd be nothing left. He shut it down and said, "You don't need to do this."

"This is for me, not you."

That might be true.

It might be payment, too, or at least have a payment component to it.

"Next time," he said.

She licked his ear and wiggled on him.

"Come on."

"I will, but next time," he said.

"You don't know what you're missing."

"I'm sure I don't."

"Well, if you change your mind, you know where I am."

Then she was gone.

It took him a long time to get to sleep. He kept making up arguments to support the fact that it really would be for her, not him. He almost convinced himself before finally conceding it was all a pile of crap.

He let the pounding of the storm rock him to

sleep.

When he woke the storm was no longer audible and faint rays of dawn were washing through the windows. He got up, stretched and headed for the master bedroom to get to the shower.

Atasha was in the bed.

A knife was stuck in the side of her head and the pillow was soaked in blood.

**TWO WEEKS LATER
DAY ONE**

August 13
Monday

2

There was a time when Raverly Phentappa thrived on the fame. She got a secret smile deep down inside every time a stranger recognized her on the street or shouted her name. Now she did her best to keep that fame in a bag. As she walked through the heart of Denver's financial district Monday morning, that bag consisted of oversized sunglasses, a baseball cap with an uneventful ponytail pulled through the back, a green Aero T, jean-shorts with no designer label stitched on the back and lips with no rouge.

She was just an ordinary Joe.

She pushed through the revolving doors of the cash register building, walked across an expansive vaulted lobby and entered the elevator that served floor 42, the home of Denver's most renowned criminal defense firm, Tristen & Day, P.C.

She was pretty.

In fact, Harvard law degree aside, she'd be the

first to admit that her big break came because of her face and her body. She was the island girl that sailors searched the world for and then lost all sense of judgment once they found her. Her skin was golden brown, her eyes were green and her raven hair was thick and long. Whatever her ancestry was, it worked.

At thirty, she'd accomplished a lot.

Most people knew her as CNN's legal commentator, smack in the middle of whatever criminal or legal mess happened to have its fingers around America's throat. Less people knew that she was the author of three true-crime novels that were acclaimed by readers and reviewers alike.

She got out of the elevator on floor 42 and pushed through fancy glass doors into a contemporary reception area. Denver's bare-knuckles criminal defense trial attorney, Anderson North, showed up almost immediately, introduced himself with a white smile and whisked her to a corner conference room with blue leather chairs and floor-to-ceiling windows that framed Denver below and the mountains not-so-below.

"Thanks for coming," North said. "Nice disguise."

She sat down.

The chair was soft but supportive.

"Actually, this is the reality," she said. "The disguise is what you see on TV."

He poured coffee into two cups and handed her one.

"Let me get right to the point," he said. "You have a fan but I'm not sure it's going to be one you want. It's a guy who, if he's to be believed, has killed a lot of people and isn't done yet. He's taken a liking to you."

"Is he a client of yours?"

"No."

"Then what's your source of information?"

North got somber.

"I have a good friend who's a lawyer out in L.A.," he said. "The killer is his client."

"What's your friend's name?"

North frowned.

"He's asked me to keep that confidential," he said. "Here's what's going on. His client—let's just call him Mr. K for a moment—wants to start a dialogue with a homicide detective here in Denver by the name of Nick Teffinger. Do you know him?"

No, she didn't personally.

"I know of him," she said. "I've seen him on TV. I also know this, if this guy really is a killer and actually starts a dialogue with Teffinger, then he's out of his mind. Sooner or later Teffinger will find a way to rip off his head and pee in the hole."

North smiled.

"Thanks for the visual," he said. "The fact remains, rightly or wrongly, that Mr. K wants to communicate with Teffinger. Here's the interesting part. He wants to do it through you."

The words felt like ice.

"Through me?"

North nodded.

"The way Mr. K sees it happening is that he'll communicate to his lawyer out in L.A. The communication will then be passed to me, and from me to you, and from you to Teffinger. Then vice-versa in the other direction."

"I don't get it. Why so complicated? Why doesn't he just call Teffinger up anonymously on the phone? Why does he want me in the loop?"

"Let me take those questions one at a time," North said. "First, the chain is intended to maximize the degree of separation and minimize the risk of Mr. K getting caught. It also minimizes the creation of evidence that could be used in a court of law. What we end up with is a pool of hearsay smothered under a layer of attorney-client confidentiality. Second, and more importantly, you're in the loop because Mr. K eventually wants you to memorialize him. At some point you're going to get an information dump of all his dirty little deeds—files, photos, evidence, details, the whole shebang. It may come after his death. He's making arrangements with the attorney in L.A. to get everything to you. You'll then use it to write the book of the century."

"About him."

"Right, about him," North said. "I've talked to the L.A. lawyer, who's my friend and who I trust. It's his opinion that Mr. K is not exaggerating. He may very well be the killer of the century."

"That doesn't explain why he wants me in the loop," Raverly said.

"I think that's just his way of bonding with you," North said. He sipped coffee and studied her over the edge of the cup. "I've done research on it. If all we're doing is passing communications, we're doing nothing wrong. We're not encouraging him to commit crimes, we're not becoming accessories before or after the fact, we're not aiding or abetting. We're functioning as telephones, in effect."

Raverly cocked her head.

"I don't want to encourage this guy," she said. "I don't want to make him feel like he's worth a book. Between you and me he is, but I don't want to give him the satisfaction of knowing it."

North nodded with understanding.

"There is that," he said. "That's why, if you don't want to do it, I understand. Also, there's the risk."

"Which is what?"

"Which is getting in the guy's universe," he said. "You can't pass mud along without getting some on our hands. Who knows what triggers this guy. You could end up being a target."

Raverly walked to the windows and looked down.

The flashing lights of a police car were pulling a van to the curb.

People walked, looking like gumdrops.

She knew she was going to take the assignment.

She also knew why.

It wasn't because of the book.

"Let's give it a shot," she said. "I'm curious where this is going."

3

An island girl flagged Teffinger down mid-morning on Monday as he pulled up to the department. He was in the '67 with the top down and a Beach Boys song on the radio. Above, a Colorado sun splashed down and heated the black vinyl seats.

The woman leaned in and said, "A mid-year, lucky you."

Teffinger unscrewed a thermos, topped off a disposable cup in his left hand and said, "The bank owns it. You're that reporter from CNN."

True, she was.

"Your eyes are two different colors, green and blue," she said. "You want to take me for a ride?"

He did.

He did indeed.

They ended up at Wash Park under the shade of an oak. Two gay joggers gave Coventry the once-over as they strutted past.

"I had an interesting meeting with an attorney by the name of Anderson North this morning," Raverly said.

Teffinger recognized the name.

They'd also been in the same courtroom a number of times.

North was one of only a handful of defense attorneys in town who had the chops to tip the scales of justice in the wrong direction. On the record, every prosecutor in the city hated the guy. Off the record, they admitted he'd be the one they called if they ever needed someone from the dark side.

"What do you think of him?" she asked.

Teffinger took a swallow of coffee and extended the cup to her, expecting a decline. To his surprise she took it and sipped.

"Thanks."

"No problem," he said. "North? I think he's a guy who has a job to do and does it. Personally, I wish his job was collecting trash, but I hold him no ill will."

"Good."

"Why?"

She told him.

She gave him all the details about Mr. K, his L.A. lawyer who was a friend of North's, Mr. K's desire to open up communications with Teffinger and the book component.

"Are you receptive?"

He didn't hesitate.

"Of course, assuming he's legit and not just some quack out to waste my time," he said.

"Good," she said. "He's got two things to tell you so far."

"Shoot."

"First, he's killed twenty-four people total."

"So he says."

"Right, so he says. Second, He's going to kill number twenty-five here in Denver on Wednesday night."

"Who?"

"A woman."

"What's her name?"

"He hasn't said."

"Did he say anything about her, where she works or whether she's young or old or anything like that?"

"No, not a thing."

"Why is he going to kill her?"

"He hasn't said."

"Why does he want me to know?"

"He hasn't said, but we could guess," Raverly said.

Teffinger chewed on it.

Right, they could guess, with the usual suspects being that the guy wanted to turn Teffinger into a chicken with no head for the next two-and-a-half days, or that he wanted to taunt Teffinger after the fact as to how he'd been able to pull off a murder even after giving Teffinger a warning.

"So far I'm not impressed," Teffinger said. "Tell him I don't want to hear from him again unless he can prove he's legit. Tell him to feed me a detail about one of his murders, something only the killer and the police would know, something that isn't public information. If I just want to see someone stand around and beat their own chest, I'll go watch King Kong."

She called North and relayed the request.

Then she told Teffinger, "I don't know how long it will take to get an answer."

He nodded.

He understood.

"I want you to know something," Raverly said. "If this guy turns out to be legit, it's not about the book. That's not what I'm after. What I'm after is for you to catch him. I'm only in it to be sure he gets enough rope to hang himself. The way I see it, the more he talks, the more we can figure out who he is."

Teffinger cocked his head.

"We?"

"Yeah, we. I'm your new best friend."

Two hours later, she called him.

"Got a response," she said. "First, one of

the people he killed was a woman named Ashlyn White. She was a lawyer in San Francisco and was his most recent kill. He abducted her in the underground parking lot of her office building three months ago, on May 3 to be precise. She has a Kanji tattoo on her right buttock that means, Love. He slit her throat with a box cutter and buried her three feet deep at Baker Beach in the cypress trees on the bluff. She's still there as far as he knows. He took her engagement ring and ending up giving it to his girlfriend at the time. She later left him but kept the ring."

Teffinger's heart raced.

This was detailed.

This was real.

"What else?" he asked.

"Nothing on her. He said the other victim would probably be more meaningful to you because she was from Denver. It was a woman named Booklyn Parks."

Brooklyn Parks.

The words cut with the force of jagged glass in Teffinger's brain. Brooklyn Parks was the younger sister of Evan Parks, a high school track buddy back in the day. Brooklyn had a habit of jumping on Teffinger's back and wrestling him to the ground. She was three years younger and there were lots of older girls in line before her, so what she wanted to happen never did, at least at that point in time.

They kept in touch over the years and finally, five years ago on a drunken night, everything fell into place.

When Teffinger closed his eyes he could feel the velvety touch of the woman's skin and hear the laughter in her voice.

He snapped the image out of his head and said, "What'd he say about her?"

"Are you okay?"

"Yes, what'd he say?"

"He said he abducted her in the parking lot of the Mirage in Las Vegas on September 15th of last year," she said. "He drove her out into the desert on a dirt road about thirty miles northwest of Las Vegas. Then he set her loose and let her run. He kept trying to run her over with his car until he finally got her. He dragged her body into an arroyo and left her there for the bugs and the sun."

Teffinger's hands shook.

"Where are you right now?"

"Home."

"Which is where?"

"I have a loft by Coors Field."

"I'm going to Las Vegas," he said. "Do you want to come?"

She did. She absolutely did.

"Give me your address and meet me down at street level in ten minutes."

4

It was 121 degrees in Vegas when Teffinger and Raverly landed at McCarran International Airport late Monday afternoon. A man in plain clothes and a long black ponytail intercepted them at the gate and introduced himself as homicide detective Johnnie Greywolf Dey-Keya.

Teffinger liked the man immediately.

His cheekbones were high and his teeth were white. He had the grip of a demon and the eyes of a hunter. Not unsurprisingly, those eyes fell a lot more on Raverly than they did on Teffinger.

Ten minutes after deplaning, they were whisking back into the sky in a small lime-green helicopter, heading north, with a middle-aged woman in the pilot's seat.

Dey-Keya brought them up to speed.

"It turns out that a vehicle registered to the woman you talked about, Brooklyn Parks, ended up getting towed out of the Mirage's parking lot on

October 3 after appearing to be abandoned. It went to our impound lot. I checked it after you called and didn't find anything that would suggest a struggle."

"No blood or anything like that?"

"Right," Dey-Keya said. "A case was never opened on the woman."

"So there was no missing-person investigation or homicide investigation or anything along those lines?"

"Correct. If we find her body, obviously that will change."

"What about surveillance cameras in the parking lot?"

"They don't keep the tapes that long."

Teffinger looked out the window.

They were paralleling a surreal mountain range. Unlike the Rockies, these mountains had no trees or greenery. They were barren, wind-chiseled, desolate deathtraps with no redeeming value other than an as a reminder of how inhospitable the earth could be. Rattlesnakes and scorpions might be able to live there but not much else.

Teffinger put his hand on the pilot's shoulder and said, "Don't crash."

She patted his hand.

"Haven't in over a day now," she said.

Teffinger knew she was kidding but looked at Dey-Keya just to be sure.

The man nodded.

"You crashed two days ago?"

"No, not two days ago, yesterday."

"You're messing with me," Teffinger said.

"Wish I was," she said. "They say that when you fall off the horse you need to get right back on it. What you see up here is me getting on a horse."

"How'd it happen?"

"It just dropped," she said. "It was some kind of mechanical failure." She pointed to the right. "There it is."

He looked.

Sure enough, there on the brown desert dirt was a tangled mess of charred metal with some virgin splashes of lime-green.

Dey-Keya slapped him on the back.

"You should see your face," he said.

Ten minutes later Raverly said, "That looks like a road." It wasn't much, hardly more than an occasional indentation on an otherwise clean desert pallet, but it was enough that they followed it west.

It dead-ended where the mountains started to rise.

"This has to be it," Teffinger said.

They circled in search of an arroyo or body or anything that looked like it didn't belong.

Ten minutes passed.

Nothing showed up.

"Set it down," Teffinger said.

"Are you serious?"

Ground level was the same temperature as the business end of a Cuban cigar. Heat radiated through Teffinger's soles and baked the bottoms of his feet.

He had no hat or sunglasses.

The horizon line wiggled behind a plume of rising heat.

Whatever search was to be had here wouldn't be a long one.

They split up.

Raverly headed up the road.

"Where you going?"

"If he was going to play cat and mouse with her, I don't think he would have come out this far where the terrain gets so uneven. I think he would have hung back where everything is flatter and there was less chance of getting his car stuck."

It made sense to a point.

"Maybe, but she would have run this way, trying to get to higher ground."

The heat pounded them with mean fiery fists.

The search turned up nothing.

Then Raverly shouted, "Got something!"

Teffinger pushed through the sizzle in that direction and found her standing at a slight indentation in the ground, possibly a shallow arroyo at one point but now mostly filled with dirt.

Out of that dirt stuck a hand.

It was mostly bones, long picked clean at this point, but definitely a human hand, connected no doubt to a human body beneath the surface.

Teffinger looked at Dey-Keya and said, "Are your crime lab guys any good?"

"They're the best."

"Get them out here."

5

The meticulous crime scene investigation dragged on hour after hour after hour. In the end they had a woman's body silently scooped from the dirt in a state of almost total decay. The bones from her ribcage to her skull were severely shattered, consistent with being hit by a car at high impact. Although her face was unrecognizable, the pendant around her neck wasn't.

It belonged to Brooklyn Parks.

Other than the woman's body, they found nothing. The scene didn't cough up a scintilla of evidence as to who killed the woman. There were no cigarette butts, no empty coke cans, no dislodged car parts, not a single thing of use, not from the place where the body was found all the way back to the nearest piece of asphalt.

They had a victim and not an ounce more.

At the end of it all, it was too late to catch a flight back to Denver. Teffinger and Raverly checked into separate rooms at the Cosmopolitan. Teffinger drank his weight in water, showered and laid down on the bed just to rest his eyes for a few minutes.

When he woke up it was evening.

The sun was almost gone and the city's neon was in full force.

The room had a small balcony overlooking the strip.

He stepped onto it and let a light breeze blow on his face.

Then his phone rang. It was Sydney Heatherwood, the newbie to the homicide department, one year into her adventure. Teffinger pulled up an image of a young mocha face and tight athletic body.

"I'm out here in San Francisco working with a detective by the name of Andy Peterson," she said. "He's had the crime unit and cadaver dogs working the bluffs at Baker Beach all day. We're finally hitting pay dirt, right now, even as we speak."

"You got a body?"

"We do indeed," she said. "It's buried three feet down, just like your good friend Mr. K said. It belongs to a woman but other than that I can't tell you too much about it right now."

"Good job."

"I just watched. They did all the work."

"You sound weird."

"It's winter out here," she said. "There's fog and rain and wind. I don't know who invented this place but they sure screwed it up."

Teffinger smiled.

"Figure out how the guy picked the lawyer to be his victim. Why her out of everyone in the world? Figure out if she was a wrong place wrong time girl or something more deliberate and calculated. Figure out the motive."

"I'll try."

"Thanks, I owe you one."

"One? What kind of math are you using?"

He dialed Raverly's room and said, "I'm going to go scrounge up a beer somewhere. You want to come along?"

She did.

She did indeed.

They headed north on Las Vegas Boulevard, watched the Bellagio fountains dance to a Celine Deon song, then crossed over to Paris and played the pass line at a craps table long enough to get four complimentary drinks, Bud Lights for him and screwdrivers for Raverly. He was $100 up at that point, tossed the chips on the waitress's tray as she passed and told Raverly, "Forty-eight hours."

He expected her to not understand.

She knew what he meant, however.

He was referring to the time left before Mr. K

struck Denver.

"How are you going to stop him?" she said.

"I don't know."

Outside the strip was chocked with headlights five lanes thick in both directions, moving slower than the walkers. Horns honked, motorcycles revved, drunken party voices shouted and faces hung out windows.

"You need to get North to tell you who his attorney friend is out in L.A.," Teffinger said. "Then we need to get him to tell us who his client is."

Raverly chewed on it.

Her expression wasn't enthusiastic.

"You're asking for two separate attorneys to breach their trust," she said. "I'll try but we better be working on a plan B in the meantime." A beat then, "It might be easier to follow the telephone trail. If we could get North's records, that would show who he's talking to in L.A. Then if we could get that person's records, it would show who he's talking to."

Teffinger kicked a coke can.

"Our guy's too smart to not have thought of that," he said. "He's probably using a payphone and if he is using a cell, I'm sure he's distanced himself from it. It's probably a disposable or prepaid, purchased for cash, or something of that nature. There are a hundred ways to do it. Go to Google and type in anonymous cell phone and you'll find half of them right there."

"Still, it's worth trying."

"It is and I'll set it in motion. Maybe he wants to be caught and he'll get sloppy on purpose. That's not what my gut tells me but you never know. The only thing I know for sure is that this guy is 100 percent legit and has coughed up two bodies to prove it."

Suddenly something happened that Teffinger didn't expect. Raverly grabbed his hand and held it as they walked.

"We need to get him talking some more," she said.

"I was thinking the same thing, except shouting instead of talking."

"What do you mean?"

"Talking implies control and deliberation," he said. "I need to get into his emotions and twist them. I need him to spit things out before he gets a chance to think them through."

Raverly squeezed his hand.

"The system's not built for that," she said. "There's too much back and forth."

"Exactly," Teffinger said. "That's why we need to change the system."

"Meaning what?"

"Meaning I need to start talking to him direct-ly."

"How are you going to do that? Just shut him off unless he calls you direct?"

"Maybe."

"I don't know that he'll go for it," she said. "There's another option, though. We already know he's taken a shining to me. He probably wouldn't mind talking to me as long as he felt there wasn't too much risk."

Teffinger put his arm around her waist.

"No. You're already too close to the fire."

"Screw the fire," she said.

They let themselves get soaked by the buzz of the strip. Teffinger kept his arm around the woman's waist, occasionally moving his fingers a bit.

Her muscles were taut.

"There's something you should know about me," he said.

"That sounds serious."

"It sort of is," he said. "Someone's out to kill me."

Raverly came to a stop and looked at him.

"Who?"

"I don't know," he said. "Two weeks ago I picked up this girl hitchhiking. She was broke and from out of town and just got dumped by her boy-friend. It was storming out and she was soaked and cold. I tried to get her a hotel but she had this thing about not taking charity. Finally I convinced her to at least sleep on my couch for the night."

"I remember that storm. I watched it for over an hour."

"Then you know how bad it was," Teffinger said. "My whole neighborhood was in blackout when I got home. Nice guy that I am, I talked her into taking my bed and letting me sleep on the couch. She didn't want to put me out but finally relented. When I woke up the next morning, she was dead in the bed. She'd been stabbed in the side of the head with a knife that was meant for me. Whoever did it thought they were killing me."

"Damn."

"Right, damn," he said. "I can't stop thinking about it. The poor girl, I don't even know who she was. She told me her first name—Atasha—but I never even asked her last name. She didn't have any identification her purse, no driver's license or anything. All she had was makeup, a couple of candy bars and $27.32 in cash."

"Did she say where she was from?"

"New York, on her way to Seattle," he said. "I've spent days trying to trace her with no luck."

"What a nightmare."

"Actually, it is; and I don't want it spreading in your direction," he said.

"Well, maybe I do," she said. "Do you have any idea who wants you dead?"

"Nothing concrete," he said. "The best guess is

that it relates to an old case; maybe a brother or relative of someone I ended up catching, something like that. We're pulling files but nothing's jumping up and shouting yet."

Raverly ran a finger down his cheek.

"You were all sexy out there in the desert today, sweating and everything," Raverly said. "Did I mention that before?"

Teffinger shifted his feet.

"No, you must have forgotten."

"Well bad, bad me. Let's get back to your room and I'll make it up to you."

DAY TWO

August 14
Tuesday

6

The earliest flight to Denver took off just as the Nevada sun rose over the desert. Teffinger put the armrests in a death grip and concentrated on the structural stress of the aircraft. The wheels lifted, the heavy vibration disappeared and the ground dropped away at a crazy speed.

Raverly patted his hand.

"Imagine that, you're still alive."

He grunted.

"Tomorrow's the day," he said. "I feel like time's a python and it has me in a stranglehold. The chief is going to want a full briefing. Then he's going to want to get a plan in motion for tomorrow night. That means mobilizing people, which in turn means meetings, lots and lots of meetings—meetings I don't have time for, to be precise."

"Blow them off."

"Play it out," he said. "I blow them off, the guy

takes his kill, and then I get the blame for not being a team player. On the other hand, if I can get all the noise out of my life and concentrate, I'll have a better chance of figuring out who he is. That's the key, not to blanket the city with a shotgun, but figure out who he is and introduce him to a rifle shot."

"So it comes down to whether you want to cover your ass or catch a killer."

He nodded.

"That's it, to a point. When you get right down to it, if I cover my ass all I'm doing is being selfish. I'm putting myself before the wellbeing of the next victim."

"So what are you going to do?"

"I'm going to catch him."

"No you're not," she said. "We are."

"Yeah, right. I forgot. We."

The seatbelt sign was still on. Teffinger unsnapped, got vertical and wandered back to the flight attendant's station where a startled young woman gave him a stern look.

"The seatbelt sign's on," she said.

Teffinger sat next to her.

"I need coffee."

"We'll be serving—"

He handed her a twenty.

"Do me a favor, as soon as you're authorized, get to me first and keep it topped off. Can you do that?"

She took the bill and stuffed it in her bra.

"Your eyes are two different colors," she said.

"I know," he said. "When the left one starts to turn green it means I don't have enough caffeine in my system. That's why this is so important."

She smiled.

"Is that the CNN reporter you're sitting next to? Raverly Phentappa?"

"Yes."

"I knew it."

Back in his seat Teffinger called the district attorney, Clay Pitcher, a barrel-chested man with yellow cigar teeth. He was five years from retirement and hard to get riled up at this point. After filling the man in on everything that was going on, Teffinger asked him the all-important question. "Can we get a search warrant for Anderson North's phone records?"

Clay's reaction was quick.

"No."

"No?"

"No."

"Why not?"

"Because he's not doing anything wrong," Clay said. "He's passing information but he's not committing a crime."

He hung up, looked at Raverly who had been listening to it all, and said, "Your turn."

She dialed Anderson North and caught him on his drive into work.

"I want you to tell me who your L.A. contact is," she said.

"Why?"

"Because I want to talk to him."

"About what?"

"About telling me the name of his client."

"That's a dangerous, dangerous path, and I'm not going to let you go down it," he said. "Besides, my marching orders are clear. No one's supposed to try to backdoor this guy. That means me and it also means you."

"But—"

"No buts," he said. "I've been set up to be a Chinese wall and that's exactly what I'm going to be." A beat then, "Look, even if I told you who my contact is, there's no way in hell he would ever turn in his own client. I know this sucks, but that's the way the system works and you know it."

That was true.

She did know it.

She hung up, looked at Teffinger and said, "No go."

The seatbelt sign went off. Ten seconds later the flight attendant showed up with coffee and a smile.

"Let's get that green eye back to blue," she said.

"Thank you."

Teffinger avoided the confused look on Raverly's face and lowered his voice. "When we get to Denver we'll hire a P.I. I'm getting those phone records and that's all there is to it."

Raverly nodded.

"I'll do the hiring and the paying," she said. "That will keep you one step removed."

"Thanks."

Twenty minutes later Sydney called and said, "The woman in the dirt was definitely the lawyer, Ashlyn White. Her throat was slit just like the guy said. I don't mean to be crass with what I'm about to say, but I don't think she was a random hit or a spur of the moment thing."

"Why not?"

"Like I said, I don't want to appear rude, but the woman's not a looker. She's in her mid-thirties and, well, just not all that attractive. More than that, though, she was taken late at night when the parking garage wasn't getting much activity. It wasn't a place to stroll. It was more of a place to hide and wait for someone you already picked out."

Teffinger cocked his head.

"Lawyers know things," he said. "Maybe she knew something and our friend wanted to get it out of her."

"Possibly," Sydney said. "We're also looking into robbery. The woman left the office with a briefcase. It wasn't at the grave site."

"Does anyone know what was in it?"

"Not at this point."

"Well, she's our best connection to our little friend so keep pressing. The clock's ticking."

"I understand."

7

In the 1400 block of Larimer Street, Raverly walked up a rickety wooden staircase to the second floor of a turn-of-the-century building and stepped into the office of private investigator Jack Bahamas III.

He was behind the desk studying papers, sexy as ever.

A cigarette dangled from his lips.

An overflowing ashtray sat to his right.

To his left was a cup of coffee.

He looked up, locked eyes and said, "Long time."

That was true, it was.

She'd used him once before on a very delicate, very private matter. He did his job well and kept his mouth shut. He also made her thighs tingle every time she was around him.

She hopped up on the desk and dangled her legs.

He ran an index finger in light circles on her knee and said, "Is this business or pleasure?"

"Business."

"Damn, so close—"

"Actually, sometimes you are. I need phone records," she said.

"Whose?"

"A lawyer. His name's Anderson North."

Bahamas took a deep drag and blew smoke.

"Phone records are almost impossible to get these days," he said. "You'd think they'd be the easiest thing in the world but they're not." A beat then, "If you want to know who this guy's been talking to, it's almost easier to just steal his phone."

Raverly pulled an envelope out of her purse and set it on the desk.

"I don't care how you do it," she said. "What I care about is that it gets done today."

"Today?"

She nodded and scribbled digits on a notepad.

"That's my new number. Call me the minute you have something. Needless to say, this is confidential. Keep your lips as tight as they go."

Then she was gone.

Ten minutes later she was back.

"Look, if you steal it, he can't know about it," she said. "Write down all the incoming and outgoing numbers over the last week and then slip it back where you got it."

"That's a tall drink of water," he said.

"Then get yourself thirsty."

8

Tuesday morning was a flurry of motion but whether it was forward or backwards or sideways only time would tell. Either way the basics got done. Teffinger fully briefed the chief who planned to flood the streets with overtime and bodies tomorrow night. He also called in Clay Pitcher to get warrants to obtain flight manifests into Denver for today, tomorrow and the last two weeks, to cross-reference them to flights into San Francisco and Las Vegas when the two prior murders occurred.

"It would be nice if we could cross-reference hotels too," he said.

That was true.

It would be nice.

It would also be impossible to do it that quickly.

Whether they should issue a public warning for tomorrow night was a delicate matter still under evaluation.

Mid-morning, Teffinger had a thought that wasn't too bad of one, and dialed Dr. Leigh Sandt, the FBI profiler in Quantico, Virginia, to prove it. As the phone rang he pulled up the image of a classy woman, fiftyish, with Tina Turner legs and a rock on her wedding finger the size of a small planet.

"It's me," he said. "Teffinger."

"If I had half a brain I'd hang up right now before you get to say another word," she said.

He smiled.

"Go ahead," he said. "I'll give you ten seconds."

Silence.

Then the line went dead.

A minute later his phone rang and Leigh's voice came through. "Sorry. I just had to do that."

"You had me going," he said.

"That was the plan."

He filled her in on what was happening and said, "If this guy's telling the truth that he's killed twenty-four people so far, he's got to be on your radar screen to some degree or another."

"You want me to check, don't you? That's what you want me to do."

"No, I just want you to have a nice day," he said. "The woman he's going to kill tomorrow night, though, she wouldn't mind if you checked."

Leigh exhaled.

"You fight dirty."

"Glad you noticed."

"I'll do it on one condition," she said.

"What's that?"

"Next time I'm in Denver, you take me out and get me drunk."

"Done."

He was about to punch his phone off when he heard muffled talking emerge.

"Teffinger are you still there?"

He was.

"I just had a thought," Leigh said. "Maybe the L.A. attorney doesn't really exist."

"What do you mean?"

"What I mean is, maybe the Denver attorney— what'd you say his name was?"

"North."

"Right, North," she said. "Maybe North doesn't have an L.A. contact at all. Maybe the killer is actually North's client. Maybe North just made up the part about the L.A. attorney so you wouldn't be staking out his office to see who went in and out."

He took a sip of coffee.

"You're a dangerous woman."

"So I've been told." A beat then, "I have an extension of that thought, too. Do you want to hear it?"

He did.

"Maybe North doesn't have an L.A. contact and

maybe he doesn't have a client, either."

"I don't follow."

"What I'm saying is, maybe he's the killer."

Teffinger frowned.

"This is why I never like to call you," he said. "You make my brain hurt."

He poured what was left of the coffee into the snake plant, filled up with new hot stuff. Then he headed down the stairs and north on Bannock into the guts of the city.

Fifteen minutes later he was in the heart of the financial district, leaning against a building on the shady side of Broadway with his eyes on the revolving doors that sat at the base of North's building.

Almost immediately the man emerged, walking in the direction of the 16th Street Mall.

Teffinger followed him to the burgundy awnings of Marlowe's at 16th and Glenarm, where the man disappeared inside. It was a place to see and be seen, a frequent haunt of the rich, relevant and upwardly mobile, especially lawyers. Teffinger had eaten there only twice in his life. Both times involved women he was trying to impress.

He hung outside for five minutes, deciding, and then headed in.

North was in a back corner booth with a leggy blond ten years his junior.

Teffinger slid in and said to the woman, "Can

you give us a minute in private?"

She looked at North with confusion.

He said, "Just stay put. We'll be right back."

Then he led Teffinger into the main room near the end of the bar. He put on a mean face and said, "What's going on?"

"A woman's going to die tomorrow night."

"I know that."

"How does that make you feel?"

"It makes me feel like the world's a sick place," North said. "It also makes me feel like you're trying to pressure me."

"I don't want anyone to die," Teffinger said.

"I'm sure you don't."

"If I find out you're dirty in this in any way, even a scintilla, you're going down. If I even think you're dirty, you can kiss your reputation as a defense lawyer in this town goodbye. I'll make damn sure that any client represented by you or anyone else in your firm never gets a plea deal, not even a little one. You can tell every one of your clients the minute they walk in the door that they're going to have to go to trial."

North frowned. "What do you want from me?"

"Tell me who your L.A. connection is."

"I can't do that." The man sighed. "Look, Teffinger, I know none of this is fair. I understand that it takes a lot of guts to try to shake someone like me down. I respect you for it, I really do. My advice to you is simple. I'm a conduit to the man you want. Think of the right questions. I'll pass them along and get you whatever responses come back your way. The ball is in your court, not mine. If I were you I'd spent less time trying to shake me down and more time trying to figure out how to use me. Do it through Raverly, that's the protocol. Now if you'll excuse me, I have a luncheon engagement."

Teffinger left. If North was dirty, Teffinger didn't detect it. All he could see was a man of convictions, twisted convictions, possibly, but convictions nonetheless.

He was five minutes into his walk back to homicide when he turned around and went back to Marlowe's. North was in the booth with his hand under the table on the woman's leg.

Wine glasses were in front of them, half empty.

Teffinger put his hands on the table and leaned his face into North's.

"Tell the guy no more talk. If he has something he wants to say, tell him to be a man about it and call me directly. I'm not interested in playing games with cowards." He pulled a pen out of his pocket and wrote digits on the tablecloth. "That's my number, day or night."

Then he was gone.

9

Back at homicide the chief wasn't pleased and creased every line in his 50-year-old face to prove it. "We had a direct line of communications going with the guy and you slammed it shut. What the hell were you thinking?"

"I'm tired of playing games."

"That's your answer?"

Teffinger headed for the coffee pot, filled up and took a sip.

"Good stuff," he said.

"Teffinger—"

"He'll call."

"You don't know that."

"Yes, I do." He exhaled and said, "We don't have time to do things by the book. I got a gut instinct and I acted on it and now it's done. This guy wants to dance. Trust me, the music hasn't stopped playing."

The chief scrunched his face.

"I don't even know what the hell that means."

Teffinger smiled.

"Neither do I. It sounded pretty good though, didn't it?"

Teffinger's desk was in the main homicide room, an ordinary cubical with a squeaky vinyl chair and a view out the window to the bail bond houses across the street, painted in cartoon colors. His predecessor had a real office, one with a door that shut and got as quiet as a tomb if you wanted it to. Teffinger could have had it when he was promoted to the head of homicide three years ago.

He even tried it out for two days.

The walls were a vice.

The stillness of the air was a crypt.

In the evening after everyone left, he scooped up all his papers and reclaimed his old spot. He told everyone it was because it was closer to the coffee pot, but when they paced it off it was actually three steps farther.

He didn't care.

He could breathe there.

Right now, he paced next to the window, throwing mean glances at his cell phone sitting there in the middle of his desk, as if he could will it to ring by sheer willpower.

It didn't ring.

Minute after minute after minute passed and it didn't ring.

Then one of the detectives from the property division walked into the room, a non-confrontational woman by the name of Joanne Lee who'd been given the dubious assignment of going through Teffinger's old cases to see if anyone popped out as having a motive to murder him, over and above the ordinary.

"I've been concentrating on release records," she said, referring to felons who recently got paroled. "There's none with your name tattooed on their forehead, at least that I can see."

He nodded.

He also didn't care.

Sure, he was a target, but things had been calm for two weeks, not to mention he had bigger things on his mind.

"I did find one thing of interest, though," she said.

Teffinger cocked his head.

"Go on."

"Well, do you remember that guy you killed with your hands last year."

Teffinger winced.

He remembered.

Everyone remembered.

Teffinger had been tailing the guy in connection with three recent murders. A confrontation erupted and Teffinger defended himself, choking the man to death with his bare hands in the process. Afterwards, they found out he was the wrong man.

The killing was ruled justifiable and Teffinger was cleared following an investigation. Still, deep down in his bones in the middle of the night when no one was looking, he had to admit that he probably could have backed off.

"I remember him," he said.

"Well, get this," Joanne said. "Somehow Raverly Phentappa is connected to him. She's that hot little CNN gal that everyone drools over."

The words dropped with the weight of a planet.

"You're kidding, right?"

No, she wasn't.

She wasn't kidding at all.

"How's she connected?"

"I don't know exactly," she said. "She was at his funeral though." She handed Teffinger a photo and said, "See, that's her right there. Do you recognize her?"

He did.

Just like that the ceiling was too low, the windows were too small and the walls were too close. He needed air and needed it now.

Outside he walked at a maniac pace.

The sun beat down and soaked into every pore of asphalt and wood and plant and bug and dog in the city.

It sucked the juice out of Teffinger's body.

He didn't care.

He had a question on his mind.

Was Raverly the one who tried to kill him?

Was she avenging Rekker's death for some un-known reason?

His phone rang.

A man's voice came through, one he didn't rec-ognize.

"You wanted me to talk to me," the man said. "So here I am."

"I'm not in the mood right now," Teffinger said.

He hurled the phone at a telephone pole.

It hit and shattered.

10

Back at homicide he headed up to forensics and dumped the contents of his cell phone on Paul Kwak's desk next to a bag of celery and carrots.

"What's with the rabbit food?"

"It's the wife's idea," Kwak said. "She says I'm getting fat?"

"Getting?"

"Not funny. It turns out these are actually negative calories. It takes more calories to chew them than you get."

"Well, be careful you don't disappear altogether. Someone called me on that cell phone a half hour ago. See if you can find out who."

Kwak gave it a curious stare.

"What happened to it?"

"It dropped out of my pocket."

"Were you in a plane at the time?"

"Yeah, let's say that."

"Oh, by the way, you still have that '67, right?"

Yes, he did.

"I know a guy who's looking for one."

"Mine's not for sale."

"If you change your mind let me know."

"Tell the guy he can buy my first son after he's born. That car is staying in my garage, though."

He got a new cell phone and had the old number forwarded to it. Then he called Sydney, who'd left him three messages.

"Okay," she said, "Ashlyn White was a senior associate in Petcher & Sands, which is San Francisco's biggest law firm. We're operating under the assumption that her death was somehow connected to her law practice. Right now we have three detectives down here at the firm interviewing every single employee."

"How many is that?"

"Close to three hundred, including support staff," she said. "So far no one has much to say about Ashlyn other than she was a great person and they're totally baffled. There's a lot of whispering going on about one of the uppity-ups though, a senior partner by the name of Austin Bent."

"What kind of whispering?"

"The kind that suggests he might be involved in something heavy."

"Like what?"

"Unknown."

"So what's your theory? That he killed Ashlyn?"

"That's possible; or even more possible, he might have hired someone to kill her," she said. "Maybe Ashlyn found out something she wasn't supposed to. Maybe she was going to turn it over to the police."

"That's speculation," Teffinger said.

"Yeah, but it's speculation that fits," she said. "Assume for the moment that Bent hired somebody to kill Ashlyn and assume that person who killed her is the Mr. K you've been talking to, which is just about certain given that he knew where the body was. What that means is that Mr. K is a killer for hire."

"An assassin?"

"Use whatever word you want," she said. "The bottom line is that the woman he's going to strike in Denver tomorrow night is someone prearranged, someone he's getting paid to hit."

Teffinger scratched his head.

It made sense but it didn't quite fit.

What was wrong?

Then it came to him.

"Part of his other history is Brooklyn Parks," he said. "I've known her since high school. There's no way she would ever be a hit. She was just your basic nice person through and through."

"That doesn't mean she wasn't a hit," she said.

"Anyone can become a hit. She could have seen something she shouldn't have. Someone might have told her something. She might have had a secret life. You never know."

Teffinger frowned.

"He ran her over out in the desert," he said. "That's not the way a hit goes down. That was fun."

"Well, maybe we're both right. Maybe he's an assassin who also kills on the side for kicks."

Teffinger chewed on it.

Then he said, "See if you can find out who Bent was talking to prior to Ashlyn's murder. I'm starting to think you're right in that Mr. K may very well be on that list."

11

The emotion of the afternoon burned off and got replaced with a silent sense of doom as the day waned on and the evening crept in. Hurling the cell phone into the telephone pole was now something Teffinger would take back a hundred times if he could.

Raverly called North every half hour throughout the day.

The man never answered.

When she called the firm directly, she was told North was out of the office for the rest of the day. She left messages for him to call.

He never did.

They were in homicide, Teffinger and Raverly. Everyone else was gone. Outside the twilight was growing ever deeper and now teetered on the edge of night. The windows were almost full black. They had microwave spaghetti in their guts and dirty forks in the sink.

Teffinger needed a beer but the room was a security blanket. Going home meant the day was over. Staying here meant it wasn't.

He slumped back in his chair.

"It's my fault about North," Teffinger said. "I should have never tried to intimidate him. Everything I've done in this case has been wrong."

Raverly sat on the edge of the desk.

"Not everything," she said. "There were a few moments back in Vegas that you handled pretty well."

He smiled.

Suddenly the door opened and Kwak from forensics came in. By the expression on his face the news was good.

"Got the number," he said, referring to call Teffinger so eloquently smashed into the telephone pole. "It's an L.A. number registered to Michael Decker."

"Michael Decker," Teffinger repeated.

He punched the man's name into the keyboard and got no criminal records. Then he Googled the phone number and got a hit. It appeared on the contact information for an attorney named Michel Decker.

"I thought the call came from Mr. K," he said. "It looks like it actually came from the mysterious L.A. attorney we've been looking for."

Kwak slapped him on the back.

"I'm out of here," he said. "Call me at home if you need anything."

"Thanks."

Raverly's phone rang and the voice of the private investigator Jack Bahamas III came through. "Got those phone numbers for you," he said. "I put them in a PDF format. Give me your email address."

She did.

Thirty seconds later she had the display on her phone.

"There it is," she said. "It matches your number. When you got the call this afternoon, what exactly did the guy say?"

He wrinkled his forehead.

"The best I can remember it was, You wanted me to talk to me, so here I am."

"That would be consistent with the attorney," she said. "North must have told him that you were trying to find out who he was."

Teffinger paced.

"Should I call him?"

"I don't see how it could hurt."

That was true.

His blood raced.

He grabbed Raverly by the shoulders and said, "I killed a man last year. He was a suspect in a savagely mean murder, his third across the country. I was tailing him, he spotted me and we got into a confrontation. He ended up dead. His name was Peyton Rekker. Do you know him?"

She stepped back.

"Why would you ask me that?"

"Just answer," he said. "Do you know him?"

A beat then, "No."

"No?"

"No."

"Are you sure?"

"I know of him," she said. "The case was in the papers and there were allegations of excessive force. You were cleared."

"That's right, I was cleared."

She looked into his eyes.

"Just between you and me, did they get it right?"

"Why do you want to know?"

"Do you want the truth?"

Yes, he did.

"A lot of men have tried to parade into my life over the years, Teffinger," she said. "You're the first one in a long, long time that I'm thinking about letting in."

He turned away.

She was lying to him and telling him she loved him at the same time.

The contrast hurt his brain.

"I'm going to call the lawyer," he said.

She squeezed his hand.

"Answer my question first," she said. "Did they get it right?"

He exhaled.

"They got it 70 percent right."

"Thanks."

"For what?"

"For being honest."

He raked his hair back with his finger. It immediately flopped back down over his forehead.

"It doesn't come naturally," he said. "I have to work at it."

"As long as it comes."

He dialed the L.A. lawyer, Michael Decker, who answered on the third ring.

"Why'd you call me before?" Teffinger said.

"Because you're threatening Anderson North," Decker said. "He's a mouthpiece, nothing more and nothing less. I want to be crystal clear that you understand that. He has nothing to give you so leave him alone."

Teffinger exhaled.

"Let's stop this stupid dance," he said. "Give me the name of your client and let's be done with it."

"That can't happen."

"Can't or won't?"

"Both."

"I want you to know something," Teffinger said. "Brooklyn Parks was a personal friend of mine.

I've known her since high school. What happened to her out there in the desert, it's personal to me."

The phone was silent.

Then Decker said, "I never heard of anyone named Brooklyn Parks."

"Your client never told you about her?"

"No."

"Then how'd you pass the information on to North?"

"I didn't."

"You know what I think? I think that maybe you and your client are the same person."

He hung up.

DAY THREE

August 15
Wednesday

12

Teffinger tossed all night with the equivalency of a rowboat adrift in a hurricane and paid for it with a deep exhaustion when he woke Wednesday morning. Raverly, still sleeping, hadn't killed him during the night, so he had at least that much going for him.

He didn't have energy but set out on a pre-dawn jog nonetheless, letting the cool thin air clean his lungs and wash his brain.

Today was the day.

He had a few tricks left but not many. He'd get more airline manifests today and be able to cross-reference them against San Francisco and Las Vegas. If he got a hit, maybe he'd be able to trace the name to a hotel. Most hotels had security cameras. That would give him a face to attach to the name. If the guy rented a car, he'd also have a license plate number.

Things weren't totally hopeless.

Still, the emptiness in his gut was tangible.

He felt like the smaller guy in the ring, hoping to land a sucker punch.

He ran three miles under the streetlights.

When he got back, Raverly was in the kitchen wearing a T that hung mid-thigh over bare island-girl legs, whipping up pancakes. She put her arms around his neck and said, "I've been thinking about tonight."

"And?"

"And, you're basically a good guy inside, Teffinger."

"Basically?"

"Right, basically," she said. "Don't let yourself be your own enemy tonight. If you get a chance to kill him, do it. Don't give him an inch."

"That's not the way it works."

"You know what I'm talking about."

"You get a better book if he's alive," he said. "You have a chance to pick his brain."

"Don't give him an inch," she said. "Don't even give him half an inch. The world will be a lot better off without him in it."

She poured two cups of coffee, handed one to him and said, "I've been thinking about what that L.A. attorney Michael Decker said, about him never telling North anything about Brooklyn Parks."

Teffinger frowned.

"He was just screwing with me."

"Maybe he wasn't," she said. "Maybe he was telling the truth."

"How could he be?"

"Okay," she said, "it goes like this. You wanted details on a murder, right? So you had a sense that this guy was really legit—"

Teffinger took a sip.

It was hot.

It was heaven.

"Right."

"Okay," she said. "What if Decker told North only about one murder, namely Ashlyn White, which would be enough to prove Mr. K's pedigree."

"But—"

"Hear me out," she said. "What if North is the one who killed Brooklyn Parks?"

"North?"

"Right, think it through," she said. "Here North is, in a position where he's feeding information to a detective from a killer who's owning up to murders. All he had to do was slip in information on a second murder—one done by him—and let you think Mr. K was confessing to it. That gets North off the hook."

Teffinger grabbed plates out the cupboard and set the table.

"So he was framing Mr. K, that's what you're

saying."

"Precisely. The more I think about it, the more it fits," she said. "Maybe when you rattled North yesterday you had a bigger effect than you realized. Maybe that's why he never called me back. Maybe he's feeling trapped."

She slid pancakes onto the plates.

Teffinger smothered them with strawberries and whipped cream and sunk in.

"I don't know," he said. "The problem is that Brooklyn was just a hand sticking out of the dirt. No one was going to ever find her by accident. Hell, even looking for her, it took us a long time and a truckload of luck."

"Yeah, but North wouldn't necessarily know that," she said. "He dumped the body—when?—almost a year ago, in September of last year. He never went back to it. He didn't know it got covered up." She speared a strawberry with her fork and brought it to Teffinger's mouth. "That explains why Ashlyn White was an assassination out in San Francisco but Brooklyn Parks was more in the nature of a fun kill. It wasn't the product of one guy with two dimensions, it was the product two different guys."

The words stuck.

They made sense.

"Damn it, you might be right."

"Don't do that," she said.

"Do what?"

"Put that look of surprise on your face at the same time you're saying I'm right."

He kissed her.

"Did I do that?"

"Yes you did."

"I'll say I'm sorry later."

"I'll be waiting for it."

Teffinger took a big bite, chewed and washed it down with coffee.

Tonight's kill would be pre-arranged.

It wouldn't be for fun.

He was fairly sure of that before but now he was certain.

At the office, he got a call he didn't expect, namely the Lakewood detective, Brad Bradley, who was working the murder of Atasha that took place in Teffinger's bed two weeks ago.

"Did she seem suicidal?" the man asked.

Teffinger reflected back.

"She was down," he said. "She just got dumped by her boyfriend, she was out in the weather, she was broke and all that. She wasn't what I'd call happy but she never struck me as suicidal. Why do you ask?"

"We stumbled across a secret compartment in her purse," Bradley said. "We found a small vial of liquid in there. I'm getting it tested but I'm pretty sure it's cyanide."

"Cyanide?"

"Right."

Teffinger cocked his head.

"Maybe that's how we can identify her," he said. "Check some of the mental health places out in New York. Maybe they're run across her."

"That's exactly what I was thinking. Remember, though, I'm not positive what it is. It might be some kind of weird New York drug that we bumpkins out here in Colorado never came across before."

"Take a hit of it," Teffinger said. "See if you die or get nutty as a squirrel."

"Thanks for the suggestion."

"No worries. It's the least I can do, and that's what I always do."

13

Teffinger shouldn't be worried about personal issues with the witching hour so close, he knew that, but he couldn't stop thinking about Raverly and, the more he did, the bigger her lie grew. He couldn't help but think that maybe, just maybe, she was the one who tried to kill him two weeks ago and got Atasha instead.

He could feel it in his gut.

It was settling into his bones like some kind of a creeping disease.

He had no future with her.

It wasn't surprising.

Every time without exception that he thought he'd finally found the one he'd been looking for, something always happened.

He was cursed.

He didn't know why but did know that he was.

The afternoon dragged.

Airline manifests came in but nothing cross-referenced. They took to running background checks on every single person coming into Denver. Shady characters emerged but none were of the stature they were looking for.

"He's driving in," Teffinger said.

"Maybe not."

"He is, trust me."

Who in Denver warranted an assassination?

That was the question.

If they could figure out who the target was they'd be halfway to catching the guy.

Raverly's words rang in Teffinger's ear.

Don't give him an inch.

Don't even give him half an inch.

That implied contact.

It implied a face-to-face square off.

At this point, Teffinger didn't see that happening.

Dark-bellied clouds rolled out of the Rockies in the late afternoon, foot soldiers with a solid army in tow.

It would storm tonight.

That would make a complicated situation even more complicated.

The day dragged on.

Nothing good happened.

Leigh Sandt called to report that she couldn't

find any shadows of the man in the FBI's files, closed or open.

Teffinger tried to shake the L.A. attorney one final time.

The man didn't budge.

"The blood's on your hands," Teffinger said.

"We both know that isn't true."

The line died.

Teffinger slumped in his chair.

It was hours until game time.

He had nothing.

Outside it started to drizzle.

14

The drizzle turned into a rain and the rain turned into a storm and the storm turned into an all-out fury with a demonic soul, battering Denver with punch after punch after punch. It was night and Teffinger had no plan other than to drive around the city randomly and hope to stumble onto something.

It was one final act of desperation.

It was an arm cocked in hopes of a sucker punch.

Raverly insisted on riding with him.

He could have resisted and probably should have. It wasn't just against protocol; it was down-right insane to let a civilian tag along on a hunt for a serial killer.

She made a point, though.

"I stuck my neck out. I earned this."

He argued but in the end couldn't deny her, so there she was sitting next to him.

His watch said 9:48.

He had coffee in his left hand.

The storm battered off the buildings, swung the streetlights and filled the windshield with waves. The wipers swung back and forth at full speed, sweeping the nightscape in and out of an eerie watercolor focus.

At least a hundred cop cars, both marked and unmarked, crisscrossed the city, all connected to central command, all poised to do whatever needed to be done.

They gave Teffinger no solace.

He said nothing.

His thoughts were braced for failure.

He could already see himself slumped in a chair at a debriefing meeting tomorrow in a room full of people second-guessing how things could have gone better.

Heading north on Broadway, he flicked the radio on, got a jingly commercial, and then punched the stations until he landed on Blondie's "Call Me."

Color me your color baby,
Color me your car.

Up ahead a woman was out in the weather pacing back and forth.

"Sex never sleeps," he said.

He drifted to the curb, flashed his badge and said, "Go home tonight, honey. It's not safe out here."

"Sure."

He pulled away and told Raverly, "She'll be back as soon as our taillights disappear."

Roll me in designer sheets,

I'll never get enough.

Raverly opened her purse and pulled something out.

"I brought a friend," she said.

It was a .38.

"Do you have a permit for that?"

"No."

"Is it registered?"

"It's registered to peace of mind."

"That's a felony, for the record."

"Duly noted, for the record."

"Wipe your prints off it and throw it out the window," he said.

"No way."

She shoved it back in her purse.

Time passed, then more time and then it was midnight.

No 911 calls had come in.

No shots had been heard.

"Maybe he chickened out," Raverly said.

"Yeah, you never know."

Those were the words that came out of Teffinger's mouth. The words in his brain though were that the man had quietly taken his mark and already slipped away. A roommate or co-worker or somebody cutting through Wash Park would stumble across the body in the morning.

Another hour passed, then another and then another.

It was three in the morning.

Every fiber in Teffinger's body ached.

His eyes drooped.

He was almost asleep at the wheel and was sick to death of turning corners and circling from one nowhere point to another.

He hated to mutter the words but he did, "It's time to give up."

Raverly squeezed his hand in silence.

Then they headed home.

DAY FOUR

August 16
Thursday

15

Teffinger had no room for lust in his heart when they got home. He was too filled with failure to even think about making love, much less doing it. He downed a beer and then slipped under the covers with Raverly at his side.

If she killed him tonight—as revenge for Rekker, or whatever—he didn't care.

Outside the storm raged.

It was almost a repeat of the night Atasha got stabbed in the head.

He closed his eyes.

He had no adrenalin left in his blood.

Sleep fell on him almost immediately.

At some point later, which could have been five minutes or five hours, a slap of thunder brought him to consciousness. He checked the clock and found he'd only been out for ten minutes.

He closed his eyes again but sleep didn't come.

Raverly was dead weight next to him, breathing deeply and rhythmically, curled in a ball.

His thoughts turned to Atasha and the fact that the poor girl may have been suicidal.

It was so sad.

It made him realize that when he thought he had things bad, he was just being a baby. Having a troubled past, getting dumped by a boyfriend out in the rain with only a handful of money in your pocket, that was bad. The things Teffinger portrayed as bad in his own life were nothing compared to that.

Atasha.

Atasha.

Atasha, suicidal but murdered.

Either way she didn't stand a chance.

Who wanted Teffinger dead?

Who killed Atasha by mistake?

The storm beat on the walls and rattled the windows.

The cyanide bothered him.

It would be a terrible way to go.

It was so deadly.

Once ingested, there was no going back.

Suddenly a strange thought popped into his head. What if it was there to kill someone else? Atasha's words rang in Teffinger's ear.

"I'll make you breakfast in the morning," she said. "What do you like?"

He swallowed what was left the can.

"If you feel like working up some pancakes, I have fresh strawberries and whipped cream."

She shook his hand.

"Deal."

Was the cyanide meant for him?

Was the whole thing that night a setup?

Was it a way to get into his house without being seen by anyone from the outside world? Is that why she resisted the offer of the hotel so violently, not because she had an aversion to charity but because her plan the whole time was to get inside his house?

His heart pounded.

It actually made sense.

Atasha had been a hit woman.

She'd come to kill Teffinger.

But if that was the case, how did she end up dead? Did a second person come to kill Teffinger too and kill her by mistake?

It made sense, at least in the abstract, but it was too coincidental. What were the chances of two hitmen coming to kill Teffinger at exactly the same time?

The chance was zero, or even less.

Life didn't work on those percentages.

But if he wasn't the target, that meant that Atasha must have been the target all along.

So what happened?

Did someone else know Atasha was going to kill Teffinger and then staked out his house until she showed up to do the deed? Did he sneak in, see Teffinger sleeping on the couch and walk right past him?

The storm pummeled down.

A whistling came from the sliding glass door at the back of the house, there for a second and just as quickly gone, almost as if it had been briefly opened. The pressure in the house had moved, Teffinger could feel the shift in the room.

He stood up silently and concentrated.

Was someone in the house?

He crept that way.

Halfway there he realized his gun was on the nightstand.

He hadn't been smart enough to pick it up.

Suddenly the black silhouette of an ominous figure came around the corner.

Teffinger swung a fist at it with every fiber of strength in his body.

A grunt came, gruff, belonging to a man.

Furious fists landed on Teffinger's face and neck and shoulders and chest. Then a slash ripped across his face. He dropped to the floor, reaching for his face as he did and already able to feel the blood leaving his body.

Suddenly the lights flicked on.

A man was standing over Teffinger cocking his arm to bring a knife down in his face.

"Don't move!"

The words came from Raverly, somewhere behind him.

The man stabbed the knife down.

Just before it tore into Teffinger's face an explosion of gunfire erupted.

The man grabbed his chest, fell backwards and dropped to the floor.

The knife stayed in his hands but his fingers loosened.

He gurgled and twitched and then stared at the ceiling with open eyes, seeing nothing.

16

Mid-morning Teffinger got a call from the L.A. attorney, Michael Decker, who said, "The word on the street is that you killed my client. Is that true?"

"Is your client's name Pretson Rail?"

"It is."

"Then it's true."

Silence, then, "He left me a briefcase to be delivered to Raverly Phentappa in the event of his death. Please have her call me to make arrangements for the transfer. She can pick it up here or I can deliver it in person to her out there."

"What's in it?"

"Details," he said. "Details of twenty-four murders." A beat then, "Warn her that it's extremely dangerous. There are fifty people out there in the world at this moment that would kill her if they knew she had it. Me too, for that matter."

"Who?"

"You name it," he said. "Lawyers, politicians, CIA … Rail was a hitman who worked for a lot of different people. Heads in high places are going to roll once all this becomes public."

Teffinger took a sip of coffee.

"Was Atasha a hitman?"

"Yes. Her full name's Atasha Severson."

"Was she assigned to kill me?"

"Yes."

"Who hired her?"

"It'll be in the notes," Decker said. "Rail was hired to kill her, which he did, two weeks ago. Then, when she didn't complete her mission, the same person who hired her in the first place hired Rail to finish the job."

"Ironic."

"Not really. There aren't that many hitmen around to draw on. It's a small pool."

"There's one thing I don't get," Teffinger said. "The mark in Denver was supposed to be a woman."

Decker chuckled.

"That just goes to show you that you can't trust a guy who murders for a living," he said. "That was a misdirect. You were the target all along." He exhaled and added, "There's one more thing. One of the heads that's going to roll once you and the FBI and everyone else in the world gets their hands on this briefcase is mine."

"You're dirty?"

"Yes. Don't worry, though, I'm still going to hand the briefcase over. It's time all this comes to an end, including my role in it. I'd like a 24-hour head start."

"Let's make it 72," Teffinger said.

"That's fair."

At noon, he picked up Raverly at her loft and drove her out to Red Rocks in the foothills. They took a stroll on a dusty path with the Colorado sun beating down.

"Did I say thanks for saving me last night?" Teffinger said.

"No."

"I will."

White gauze strapped into place with white tape covered most of the left side of his face. The cut was long but not deep.

The doctor who stitched him up was a plastic surgeon.

There would be a scar but it wouldn't be of the Frankenstein type.

The path narrowed as it wound higher into the foothills.

The earth opened into an expanse to the eastern flatlands. They could see for fifty miles.

They walked single file with Raverly in front, climbing ever higher.

"You lied to me," Teffinger said.

Raverly stopped and turned.

"About what?"

"About not knowing Peyton Rekker," he said. "You went to his funeral."

She tensed, as if caught.

Then she softened.

"I didn't know him," she said. "I went there with a friend of his. I knew her. I was there to support her. That was it."

"You should have said that back when I brought it up."

"I didn't see the need."

They walked in silence.

Several magpies sat in a pinion pine.

Yellow butterflies dotted the grasses and bushes.

Raverly stopped and turned.

"You were right that I lied to you," she said. "It wasn't about knowing Peyton Rekker though. I'm going to tell you something horrible. You're going to despise me and then we're going to split up. It's better that it happens now than later."

Teffinger's blood raced.

The woman was serious.

The stress was etched on her face.

"Go on," he said.

She looked at the horizon, then at him. "I had

a boyfriend last year by the name of Robert Wicks. We were headed to Las Vegas. I was driving, traffic was almost non-existent and I was paying more attention to the radio than the road. There was a car up ahead on the shoulder. A woman was changing a tire on the street side, slightly on the road but not by much. I didn't see her until the last second. I swerved but it was too late and I ended up hitting her. It was Brooklyn Parks."

"Brooklyn?"

She nodded.

"We were scared as hell," she said. "We put her in the truck of our car and fixed her tire. Then we dumped her body in an arroyo way off the beaten path. Robert drove her car into Vegas and we ditched it in the north 40 of the Mirage's parking lot."

Teffinger stared at her.

He had no words.

"When I was passing you the message of Ashlyn White's murder, I made a spur of the moment decision and threw in Brooklyn Parks. Later, you were trying to get to Michael Decker to talk to him. I was scared if you did, you'd find out that he didn't know anything about Brooklyn. That's why I took the lead in hiring the private investigator. If he found out who North's connection was, I was going to keep it from you. You found out on your own through Paul Kwak, so at that point I had nothing to lose by showing you what the investigator found as well." She held his hand. "I was scared, Teffinger. I was scared and trapped and didn't want to lose you before I even had you."

Teffinger shook his head.

Then he turned and walked.

"Teffinger!"

He didn't stop.

"Nick!"

He kept going.

17

Teffinger left the Tundra at the trailhead with the keys in the ignition and hitchhiked back to Denver. He didn't call Raverly all day and she didn't call him.

He went home after work, made a sandwich then sat in the '67 and drank beer.

Twilight came.

Night followed.

He couldn't keep the rage up.

It was waning in spite of his best efforts.

Raverly killed Brooklyn but it had been an accident. What she did afterwards was wrong, extremely wrong, but it was the product of fear. Teffinger had done some pretty extreme things in his own life based on fear.

He was hardly one to throw stones.

Also, Raverly lied to him about Brooklyn.

To her credit, though, she told him the truth afterwards when she could have kept her mouth shut.

That counted for something.

He swallowed what was left in the blue can, crushed in it his fist and dropped it to the garage floor.

He extracted soldier number seven from a small cooler in the back seat, popped the top and took a long swallow. It wasn't as good as the first one but it was still pretty damn good.

He pulled his cell phone out of his shirt pocket and stared at it, deciding.

Then he called Raverly and said, ""You deserve better than what I gave you. I'm sorry. "

She paused and said, "Likewise. Where are you?"

"Home, sitting in my car, getting drunk."

"You want me to come over?"

The words felt like sunshine on his face.

It was going to be all right.

Everything was going to be all right.

"Yes," he said. "Yes, yes, yes."

NIGHT LAWYERS

R.J. JAGGER

DAY ONE

June 4
Sunday

1

Nick Teffinger, the 34-year-old head of Denver's homicide unit, emerged from a deep unconsciousness to find he was behind the wheel of his pickup truck in the driveway. The ache in his body indicated he'd been there all night. Streetlights still burned but the first taste of dawn was starting to beat the night away.

He shifted his six-two frame.

The movement set off hammers inside his skull and pitched his stomach into a typhoon churn.

He was on the wrong end of a serious night of drinking.

Last night was a blur.

He remembered beers and shots of Tequila and his hands up the skirt of a curvy little raven-haired thing in a shadowy booth in the back corner of D-Drop.

What was her name?

He couldn't remember.

He didn't remember leaving.

He didn't remember driving her home.

The light inside the cab wasn't much but it was enough to tell something was wrong with his hands. On closer examination it turned out to be blood. His hands were bloody, not with fresh blood, with dried blood. He couldn't see or feel a wound. The pattern appeared to be more as if he'd handled something bloody.

Then his peripheral vision noticed glass in the passenger seat. It looked like a beer bottle with the bottom broken off, leaving a jagged edge.

The jags were thick with dried blood.

It was as if the glass had been stabbed into someone's gut.

His heart raced.

What happened?

He opened the door, got out and hung on for a heartbeat to get his balance. His feet wobbled. He was still half drunk. The nausea in his stomach climbed up his throat. He swallowed it down, closed the door and headed for the front steps.

At the front of the truck he found something he didn't expect; the front end was smashed in on the passenger side. The headlight was busted out. The quarter-panel was crumpled. The bumper was dented.

He must have hit something.

He didn't remember what.

He didn't remember how.

He didn't remember where.

Get the truck out of sight.

Right or wrong, that was his thought—Get the truck out of sight. He got back in the cab, punched the opener and watched the garage door rise. The garage was full. In the left bay sat the '67 Corvette. In the right bay sat an eclectic miss-match of boxes and junk. He pulled the '67 out onto the street, got the Tundra inside and closed the door.

He forced himself to drink a full glass of water to get the sandpaper off his tongue, then made his way to the front steps to see if the morning paper was there.

It was.

He brought it to the kitchen table and went through it page by page to see if there were any reports of a hit-and-run last night, or someone being run over.

If there was, he didn't spot it.

That didn't mean it didn't happen.

It could have happened but not early enough to make the print.

He headed for the bathroom and washed his hands. The dried blood turned red under the faucet and pooled in the bottom of the sink before twisting into the drain.

His prior inspection had been correct.

There were no wounds.

He stripped out of his smoke-ridden clothes and spotted blood on his shirt and pants. There were no injuries to his body. It was exhausted and hung over but otherwise intact.

A book of blue D-Drop matches fell out of his shirt pocket. On the inside handwritten in blue ink was the name Rain, followed by a 303 telephone number. Now he remembered the name of the touchy young squeeze of last night; it was Rain.

The glass of water in his gut ached with sickness.

He vomited long and hard until he had nothing left but a dry heave and a chest soaked in sweat.

Then he curled up naked in the bed under a sheet and closed his eyes.

The room spun.

2

Teffinger woke Sunday afternoon not feeling good but not feeling like wormed-over death on a stick either. The worst was behind him. By tomorrow morning when he needed to work, he'd actually be functional. He drank coffee, swore he'd never tie one on like that again as long as he lived, and checked the web for any updates on local hit-and-runs.

He found nothing.

Maybe he'd hit a pole or a barrier.

He inspected the front end closer and found no foreign paint, remnants of clothing or anything else of use.

Outside the day was nice.

He opened the front door, got a slight breeze filtering through the house and then sat on the front steps with a topped-off cup of coffee. Three houses up, at the end of the street in a dirty turn-around, a woman sat behind the wheel of an older model Mustang, something in the vintage of the mid to late '60s. Her face was stuck in a magazine and largely hidden under a baseball cap and over-sized shades. Still, she looked familiar. Teffinger went inside and silently pulled her in through a pair of Bushnell AutoFocus binoculars.

She was an attractive woman in her late twenties.

He'd definitely seen her around somewhere before.

What was she doing up there?

Occasionally someone parked there and headed off for a hike into the open space. Maybe someone did that and she was waiting for them to return.

Although it was possible, Teffinger's gut told him otherwise.

She was there because of him.

He exhaled, deciding, then topped off his coffee, filled a second cup, stepped out the front door and walked towards her.

She picked up his movement within the first few steps but didn't start the vehicle or make an effort to leave. Teffinger went over to her window and handed the cup through.

"I thought you might want this," he said.

She hesitated, then took it and said, "Thanks."

Her hair was thick, yellow-blond, long and wavy, almost a '50s style, very sexy. Ample cleavage peeked out from behind a button-down red blouse. Below that was a short white skirt riding up dangerously high on account of the way she was seated. Perfect legs stuck out, defined and tanned.

Teffinger looked around.

"Nice day."

She took a sip.

"Yes it is."

"It's a good day to spy on someone," he said.

She nodded.

"Every day's a good day for that."

"I've seen you around town."

She shrugged.

"That's inevitable."

"Why?"

"I think you know."

"Because you've been following me?"

She slipped her sunglasses off.

Her eyes were the sexiest thing Teffinger had ever seen.

"Yes. You were bound to notice sooner or later."

"And now I have."

"Right, now you have," she said.

"So what now?"

She took a sip and said, "This is good coffee."

"Glad you like it," he said. "So now that you're busted, what happens now?"

"Busted?" she said. "Getting spotted is all part

of the plan. Everything is on course."

"Is it?"

"Yes." She drained what was left in the cup and handed it to him. Then she started the engine, slipped the shades down and said, "Got to run."

Teffinger nodded.

"One question before you leave," he said. "Why are you following me?"

She smiled.

"I'll tell you what. If you can spot me again, I'll answer that question."

"You promise?"

She blew him a kiss.

"I promise."

Then she was gone.

Teffinger made a mental note of her license plate number and then made a call when he got back in the house. The plate belonged to one Neverly Cage who lived on the near east side of town, in the 1300 block of Washington.

The vehicle was a 1968.

"Nailed it," he told himself.

He logged into the department's database, punched in her name and got nothing.

He drank another cup of coffee and then dialed the handwritten number on the inside of the matchbook, the one for Rain.

The phone rang three times and dumped into a voice mail.

"Hey, it's me, Nick," he said. "Give me a call."

He wasn't in the mood to play cat and mouse but he wouldn't have time tomorrow, so he ate a slow bowl of cereal and then hopped in the '67 and headed for Neverly Cage's house. The houses had no driveways but an alley ran behind the backyards and that's where most of the owners parked.

Teffinger spotted the Mustang in a makeshift carport that looked like an affront to every building code known to man. He parked away from it in case it came down, then circled around to the sidewalk, walked up an uneven brick path and knocked on the front door.

When the woman answered Teffinger said, "I spotted you again. So now I get to find out if you're someone who holds your promises."

The woman hesitated, then pushed the screen door open and said, "Come on in."

The place was cluttered and crammed.

The walls were close and the windows were small.

A fan blew but cross-ventilation was negligible.

The woman's skirt was off and the red blouse had been swapped for a T that hung down past her ass but not by much. One wrong bend and she'd be flashing. Teffinger made an effort to keep his eyes up.

"So how long have you been following me around?"

She smiled.

"Coffee?"

He raked thick brown hair back with his fingers. It immediately fell back down over his forehead.

"Sure. Why not?"

She poured two cups and they ended up sitting on the front steps.

"To answer your questions, four months give or take." She held her hand out to shake and said, "My name's Neverly Cage, by the way. But I assume you already know that."

He shook.

"Nick Teffinger."

"Yeah, I know."

"Four months," he said. "That's pretty impressive. I've had people follow me that long before, but they were all people I owed money to. I don't owe you money, do I?"

She smiled.

"Your eyes are two different colors. One's blue and one's green. I've never seen that before."

"One of my many flaws." He took a noisy slurp. "So Neverly Cage, why have you been following me around for four months, give or take?"

"It relates to Decker Zero."

Decker Zero.

The words pulled up a memory so vivid that Teffinger felt he was actually there.

It was last July.

The sky was dark and moonless and dripped with a steady black drizzle.

The world was nothing but shadows and shapes.

Teffinger was in the Tundra, parked with the engine off in the old abandoned warehouse district down by the South Platte. A curvy little thing named Brooklyn was with him. She was wildly drunk and her skirt was hiked up to her waist. Teffinger had his lips to hers and a hand between her thighs when something strange happened.

The shadowy shape of naked woman ran past.

She was shouting.

She was frantic.

"What the hell?"

Then a man ran past, chasing the woman.

He wore clothes.

In his hand was a knife.

The next moments were a blur. Teffinger was out in the weather, running through the dark with every molecule of force he had, shouting, "Stop!"

By the time Teffinger closed the gap, the man had the woman on the ground. One hand gripped her hair with an iron fist. The other held a blade to her throat.

Teffinger stopped five steps short and said,

"Let's everyone calm down."

The man said nothing.

"Help me!" the woman said.

Teffinger didn't move.

"Just back off," he said. "I'll let you go."

Silence.

"Just back off and go home. No one's going to hurt you."

Suddenly the man's arm moved.

The woman gargled and went limp.

Then the man ran.

Teffinger charged after him.

The gap closed and he got a punch to the back of the man's head.

They both went down.

In that split second Teffinger got a look at the face.

It was someone he knew.

It was a guy named Decker Zero.

Then a punch landed to his head with the force of a freight train and colors exploded inside his skull.

What followed was uneventful.

The woman was dead.

They never found out who she was. To this day she was still Jane Doe.

The scene produced no circumstantial evidence.

They found no fibers, no fingerprints and no

other evidence. They never found the woman's clothes. They never figured out where she had been before suddenly emerging in the shadows.

Decker Zero didn't show up at his house for over two weeks. When he did, people were waiting for him. Right now he was in custody, waiting for trial.

That was scheduled for next week.

He shook off the memory, looked at Neverly and said, "What about Decker Zero?"

"I work for Silke Jopp," the woman said.

Teffinger knew the name and knew it well.

She was a bare-knuckles criminal defense attorney reputed to be Denver's best, with a string of high profile notches in her belt.

She was defending Zero.

"So what do you do for Silke Jopp?"

Neverly ran a finger down Teffinger's arm.

"I get dirt on you," she said. "What do you think?"

He nodded. It made sense.

The prosecution's entire case was built on Teffinger's testimony. If the defense could discredit him, they could win.

"So how's that going for you?" he asked.

"To be honest it was pretty bleak," she said. "All that changed last night, as I'm sure you're aware."

DAY TWO

June 5
Monday

3

onday morning Teffinger got up before dawn, jogged under the streetlights until he ran out of air, and then headed to work in the '67 while the Tundra stayed silently hidden in the garage. He had a bowl of cereal in his lap, a spoon in his right hand and a cup of coffee in his left, steering with his knees and heading east on the 6th Avenue freeway. The sun lifted off the horizon and blinded him as best it could. He searched around for sunglasses for a few heartbeats before remembering he sat on them last week.

Neverly Cage had dirt on him.

She'd followed him to D-Drop and snapped picture after picture of him in a shadowy back booth with a woman, Rain, getting sloppy drunk and sinfully touchy. By the end of the evening the woman actually had her panties off. Teffinger's hand was under her skirt, getting busy, getting very busy if the expression on the woman's face was to be believed.

That wasn't the worst of it though.

The worst of it was the two of them leaving the bar, staggering to Teffinger's truck, then driving away crazy drunk and sideswiping a parked car en route.

That's where the dirt stopped.

"I'd love to have known what happened after that, but my car was on the other side of the bar," Neverly said. "By the time I got to it and gave chase, you were gone."

"Too bad."

"Yeah, I know. So why don't you fill in the blanks? What happened after the two of you left?"

"Use your imagination."

She ran her fingers through his hair.

"Come on," she said. "The jury is going to want to know."

"None of this will get into evidence," Teffinger said. "It has nothing to do with Zero killing someone."

The woman smiled.

It was slightly crooked and hypnotically sexy.

"You don't get it, do you?" she said. "Zero's not the one on trial. You are."

He opened his mouth to argue.

No words came out.

What she said was true. The trial would be all about

whether Teffinger's testimony was trustworthy. Now that he was a drunk, a womanizer and an intoxicated driver, maybe he wasn't so much of an upstanding citizen who could point-blank be trusted.

"Zero killed the woman," Teffinger said. "I saw it with my own two eyes."

"You saw someone," Neverly said. "Whether it was Zero or not is the question."

"It was Zero."

"That will be for the jury to decide."

"Maybe," Teffinger said. "But what you need to understand is that you succeed, all you'll do is get a guilty man off the hook."

"Spare me the boy scout talk," Neverly said. "It was dark out, you had rain in your eyes, the man's face was dripping wet and etched with fight, and you only saw it for a heartbeat, and even that was in the middle of an adrenalin rage. You weren't exactly sitting back and drawing a nice quiet sketch at that point in time."

"It was Zero."

"Was it?"

"Yes."

"What if it wasn't?"

"It was."

"So you say but what if you're wrong? What if what I'm doing isn't getting a guilty man off the hook? What if what I'm doing is keeping an innocent man out of prison? What if you're the one on the wrong side of things and not me?"

That was yesterday.

Now, this morning, he was just passing Federal Boulevard when an email landed on his phone regarding "Exhibit A." It was from Neverly Cage with a short message, "Happy viewing."

Several photographs from Saturday night were attached.

Teffinger winced.

The woman had shown them to him yesterday, but having them land right here in his own phone gave them an eerie reality.

He'd have to show them to the chief and the D.A.

It wouldn't be pretty.

More than that, he might have given the defense what it needed to make Zero a free man. If that happened, some other woman would end up dead down the road. The blood would be on Teffinger's hands.

Suddenly a bad thought entered his mind.

What if Neverly was right and he was wrong? What if he was mistaken about Zero being the guy?

He shook it off.

"Don't open that door."

Mid-morning a padded envelope got hand-delivered to the front desk downstairs by a cabbie. On it was a label with typed words:

Detective Nick Teffinger

Personal & Confidential

Inside was a CD in a clear plastic case. Although the CD itself had no markings on it, an attached yellow post-it had the typed words:

Watch this in private

Teffinger twisted the case around in his hand.

Sydney Heatherwood walked into the room, poured a cup of caffeine and plopped her athletic African-American body into the worn vinyl chair in front of Teffinger's desk. "Let me guess what your weekend was like," she said. "Blond, blue eyes, tanned legs …"

He smiled.

"Something like that."

"You never go for the black girls," she said.

"I bounced a quarter off your ass once. If I recall right, it snapped up and almost broke the ceiling light."

She punched his arm.

"You know what I mean. How come you never run down the black girls?"

"I have, three or four times."

"And?"

"And what?"

"And, how were they?"

"They were fine. I have no complaints, other

than that quarter incident." He shoved the CD in his coat pocket and said, "I got to run."

Then he was gone.

4

Teffinger headed home in the '67, picking up Neverly Cage's beat-up Mustang in the rearview mirror halfway there, three cars back and holding.

He didn't care.

Let her follow, he wasn't doing anything wrong.

He parked in the driveway.

The sun beat down.

Ordinarily he would have at least put the top up.

This time he didn't.

This time he headed straight for the front door and disappeared inside.

His heart raced.

He put the CD in the player.

What he saw he couldn't believe.

It was dark out.

A woman in a short dress had her back against a telephone pole. Her arms were stretched up above her head as high as they could go. Her wrists were tied together. A man was in the process of wrapping the rope around the pole several times and then tying it off, binding her into position.

The woman was the raven-haired beauty from Saturday night, Rain.

The man was Teffinger.

Someone was across the way, over in the deeper shadows, filming the scene with a cell phone. They were in a pickup truck. The person doing the filming had the phone hanging out the window. The lens shook and the side of the vehicle occasionally bounced into view.

A woman's voice said, "What's he doing?"

A man replied, "He's tying her up."

"Why?"

"I don't know. I think they're just screwing around."

"Forget them," she said. "Get back over here and fuck me."

"Hold on a minute."

"Preston—"

"Just a minute."

Over to the left of the frame, the back end of Teffinger's pickup was parked in view.

The license plate was readable.

It was his.

He paused the CD, stepped to the front window

and peered out around the edge of the covering. Neverly Cage was coming up the street. Teffinger watched as she headed to the end of the asphalt, turned around and then parked with the front end of the Mustang pointed at his house.

She wore the same sunglasses as yesterday.

He waited for a few heartbeats to see if she had plans to get out and walk over.

She didn't.

She just sat there with her face pointed in his direction.

He let the blinds fall back into place and then pressed Play.

The CD sprang back to life.

Teffinger kissed the woman and ran his hands up and down her body.

She responded nicely.

Her feet stretched apart of her own volition

"He owns her," the man said. "This is cool."

"Let them be," she woman said. "Turn that thing off and get back in here."

"Just a minute. I want to see what he does next."

Teffinger ripped the woman's dress down the front, exposing a taut stomach and small white panties.

"There goes twenty bucks," the man said.

Then he ripped her bra off.

"Make it twenty five."

Perky tits bounced out.

Teffinger sucked a nipple, then the other. His hand went between the woman's legs, rubbing up and down and back and forth. Then he bent down and picked something off the ground.

It was an old beer bottle.

He broke the bottom end off on the ground and then cut the woman's panties off with the jagged edge.

With the broken glass still in hand, he kissed her, long and deep and hard.

Then something happened he didn't expect.

He slapped her face.

"Fuck! Did you see that?"

He walked around her, eyeing her with predator eyes, then slapped her face again.

"Damn it!"

Then he did it again.

Suddenly the camera angle swept to the ground, as if the man was getting out of the truck. The camera got set on the hood. The jerky motion stopped.

"Preston! Get back in here!"

"This is fucked up," he said.

The audio rolled and footsteps sounded.

Then the man shouted, "Hey, asshole, leave her alone!"

"Back off."

"I said leave her alone!"

"Back off. This is none of your business."

Suddenly the camera came off the hood.

The woman had it now, swinging it towards the scene.

Teffinger and the man were closing in on each other. Teffinger had the broken bottle in hand.

The woman screamed.

"Preston!"

The cell phone fell to the ground.

The screen went black.

Teffinger slumped onto the couch and buried his face in his hands. Even seeing it, he still didn't affirmatively have any cognitive recollection of the events.

It was him though.

There was absolutely and without question not a scintilla of doubt about that.

It was him, out of his mind.

A knock came at the front door. He opened up to find Neverly Cage standing there with her hands on her hips.

"You're supposed to bring me coffee," she said.

Teffinger knew he should smile but couldn't. Based on her expression, plus the fact that she already said she hadn't followed him last night, she wasn't the one who sent him the CD.

"Sorry about that. Come on in."

"Are you okay?"

"Yeah, always."

5

Teffinger's house had a mountain where the backyard should be. Halfway up that mountain on his property was a redwood deck that sat slightly higher than the roofline of the house and offered an unobstructed view of Denver and the eastern flatlands. That's where he ended up with Neverly, drinking coffee. As far as Teffinger could tell the woman was there for two reasons; one, to try to wedge dirt out of him; and two, to be around him just because she wanted to.

"Off the record," she said, "watching you Saturday night got me a little worked up."

"Next time come over and join us."

"Next time I will."

She wasn't dressed up.

She had the look of someone who could step into a pickup game of baseball and wouldn't be afraid to slide into second.

"Have you told Silke Jopp about Saturday night

yet?"

No.

She hadn't.

"I have a meeting with her this afternoon."

"Why don't you hold off?"

"Why?"

"Because there's more to that night than what you saw."

"Like what?"

"I'm still trying to figure it out," he said. "I'll make a deal with you. Hold off until I can figure it out. If you do that, I'll fill you in on the balance."

"You're trying to figure it out?"

He nodded.

"So you don't remember?"

"Correct."

She shrugged.

"It doesn't surprise me," she said. "By my count you had seven beers and seven shots, plus the round that I sent over."

"You sent over a round?"

She smiled.

"Had to."

"Why?"

"It seemed like the right thing to do," she said. "If I'd have known you were going to drive drunk and smash into someone's car I wouldn't have done it. So how are you going to figure out the rest of the night?"

"Detect," he said. "That's what detectives do."

She studied him.

"My allegiance is with Silke Jopp," she said. "She's paying me to do a job and I'm going to do that job. On top of that, a man's life is in the balance."

"If you turn everything over right now, that might be all you ever get," he said. "Maybe it will end up being enough, but maybe it won't. If you take my way, you may end up with more. You probably will in fact."

She chewed on it.

"Just hold off for 48 hours," he added.

She sipped coffee and studied him over the edge of the cup.

"How do I know you'll actually tell me anything?"

He raked his fingers back with his hair.

"Even if I don't, in 48 hours you'll still have everything you have now. What's the harm?"

She looked out at the horizon line.

"Nice day."

"Do we have a deal?"

She frowned.

"No."

They headed down the mountain on red flagstone steps with Neverly in the lead.

Suddenly she froze.

Teffinger saw the problem.

The woman's foot had come down next to a thick rattlesnake.

"Don't move!" he said.

She said nothing.

Sweat ran down her face.

Teffinger walked around the snake, got a stick and waved it gently in front of the reptile's head until it saw nothing else.

The body coiled.

The head came up.

The tail shook.

The eyes pointed at Teffinger and away from Neverly.

"Okay, talk a slow step back," he said.

Neverly complied, getting three feet away and then running back up to the deck.

Teffinger tossed the stick down, backed up and said, "Go away. No one's going to hurt you."

The snake stayed coiled for a few heartbeats and then slithered into the brush.

"Okay," Neverly said.

"Okay what?"

"Okay, forty-eight hours."

6

The call Teffinger knew would come sooner or later came mid-afternoon, after he had sufficient time to sweat. "Seen any good movies lately?" Teffinger recognized the voice as the same one as on the tape, "Preston's."

"Cut to the chase," Teffinger said. "What do you want?"

"Whoa, whoa, whoa," the man said. "We'll get to all that. First, I want to be sure you understand the full extent of what we have."

"I've watched it."

"Right, I suspect you have," the man said. "But I want to be sure you appreciate that I didn't leave after our little fight. You thought I did, but I hung back in the shadows and saw what you did. My girl did too. We both saw it."

"Saw what?"

"Don't play games," the man said.

"Tell me," Teffinger said. "Tell me exactly what

you saw."

"We saw what you did, you little shit. You slit the woman's throat open with that little broken-bottle friend of yours; the same little friend you tried to shove into my face. We saw you throw her body in the back of your little white pickup truck. We saw you take off like a bat out of hell." A pause then, "Reminds you of the Meatloaf song, doesn't it?"

"Bullshit."

"Where'd you dump her?"

"You saw nothing because nothing happened."

"She's going to show up," the man said. "Was she your girlfriend or just someone you picked up in a bar?"

Teffinger paced.

The world spun.

"Where did it happen?"

The man chuckled.

"You don't remember?"

"Just tell me."

"The old warehouse district on the west side, near the South Platte."

Teffinger winced.

He knew the area.

He'd used it for sex more than once.

In fact that's where he spotted Decker Zero.

"So what's the bottom line?" he asked.

"The bottom line is money," the man said. "Start getting it in a pile. I'll be in touch."

The line went dead.

Thirty minutes later Teffinger was trolling through the abandoned warehouse district in second gear. The asphalt was potholed, cracked and choked with weeds. The structures were decayed, the windows were broken and pigeon wings flapped with abandon. Ten minutes into it he came to a telephone pole with a rope dangling six or seven feet off the ground. He brought the '67 to a stop and killed the engine.

His heart raced.

This was it.

This is where he killed the woman.

The rope was long and had years and years of weather and dirt. Right now it was looped around the pole multiple times, seven feet off the ground, and tied in a double square knot. The end hung limp, no longer attached to the woman's wrists.

Dried blood was on the ground.

Teffinger pictured it squirting out of the woman's neck and rolling down her chest and stomach and legs. He stooped down and picked up a white button with splats of dried blood, no doubt dislodged from her dress when he ripped it open.

He shoved it in his pocket.

He walked across the road to where the videotape was taken.

The scene from that angle was exactly as he saw

it.

This was definitely the right place.

He walked over to where the Tundra was parked in the videotape.

There were droppings of blood on the asphalt from the pole to where the bed of the truck had been. He pictured carrying the woman in his arms.

That's how he got the blood on his hands and shirt and pants.

Where did he dump her?

He'd been too screwed up to dig a grave, not to mention he didn't have a shovel. He put her in the truck and took her somewhere, probably with intent to get her away from the immediate scene but maybe not without much more thought than that.

Maybe he only went a hundred yards or so.

Maybe he dragged her into a structure or dumped her in the first old rusted trash bin that came up. That would have been smarter than driving around town with a body in the back.

Had he been at least that coherent?

He untied the rope and brought it with him as he headed down the asphalt on foot. The blackmailer, Preston, hadn't said anything about seeing Teffinger stop anywhere in the vicinity after putting the woman in the truck. He must have made it at least out of visual range before stopping, assuming that's what he did.

The asphalt curved.

He walked until he was out of range and then looked in earnest for a place that might have attracted him Saturday night.

He came to a dilapidated brick structure, four or five stories high that might have been a small manufacturing plant back in the day. The steel man-door in front was secured with a rusty padlock. Red spray paint said, "No Trespassing." To the left was a rollup delivery door that was raised up two-feet, leaving a gap at the bottom. Teffinger tried to muscle it up and found it solidly stuck.

He looked around, saw no one, then got down on the ground and worked his way inside through the gap. It was dark. The structure had few windows and those that existed were boarded.

The air had a pungent glue-like odor, maybe the ghosts of chemicals used to make rubber parts.

There was no body on the ground.

If Teffinger dragged the woman in here, he wouldn't have pulled her far. He took three steps into the darkness just to be sure he wasn't missing anything.

A dark silhouette ten feet farther in caught his peripheral vision.

It looked like a body.

7

So what are we doing in here?" The words came from behind Teffinger. They belonged to Neverly. She was already through the gap and getting to her feet, nothing more than a black silhouette.

Teffinger walked towards her.

"What are you doing here?"

"I'm working," she said. "I saw you take the rope off that pole. What's it relate to?"

"A case."

"Which one?"

"One that doesn't concern you." He got down, rolled out the gap and said, "Come on."

It worked.

The woman followed him.

From where she had been inside, she probably wouldn't have been able to see the silhouette on the floor, not to mention that her eyes hadn't adjusted yet. Now he needed to make sure she left the area.

"I'm starved," he said. "You want to get a bite?"

She did.

She did indeed.

They ended up at a red vinyl booth at Wong's on Court Street, sipping tea and munching egg rolls. "This is a weird situation," he said. "You're the enemy but I'll be honest with you, every time I look into your eyes all I want to do is throw you up on this table and rip your clothes off."

She smiled, slightly crooked, seriously sexy.

"They probably have rules against that."

He nodded.

"They probably do."

"You're a rule-breaker though, Teffinger," she said. "We both know that."

"Me? Not really—"

She cut a slice of egg roll, speared it with her fork and brought it to Teffinger's mouth. He took it, chewed and said, "So how is this going to end?"

She shrugged.

"That depends on how good your memory is."

"Which means what?"

"Which means the person I work for has some stuff on you," she said, "or, to be more precise, will have some stuff in 48 hours."

"Less than that, actually."

She smiled.

"That's true. The only value to that stuff is if you testify at trial. Now, if it turns out that your memory fades before the trial and you're not really sure if Zero is the person you saw that night, then the D.A. would drop the charges, the trial wouldn't happen and the all the stuff on you would end up in some forgotten little manila folder in some forgotten little box somewhere."

Teffinger cocked his head.

"Just for the record, you're getting awfully close to witness tampering," he said. "Another way to phrase it is obstruction of justice. That's a felony offense."

She pulled out her cell phone, flicked the screen for a moment and then handed it to him.

It was a photograph of him removing the rope from the pole.

A second photo showed him picking a button off the ground.

A third showed him rolling under the gap.

"You're very photogenic," she said.

He handed the phone back to her.

"I do what I can."

"These weren't taken with my phone," she said. "I have a digital camera with a good zoom. I download the pictures to my computer and then email copies to myself as well. That way they're in a bunch of places and can't get lost."

He took a sip of tea, put a serious expression on his face and said, "I need you to stop following me for a day."

"Why?"

"There are things I need to get done."

She chewed on it.

"What's it worth to you?"

"You name it."

She defaulted to a blank stare, then refocused and looked into his eyes.

"Tomorrow night, you take me out," she said.

"Where?"

"Wherever I want."

He clinked his cup against hers.

"Deal, but no tricks. I don't want to see you in my rearview mirror."

"You won't."

8

Teffinger had $6,728 in his savings account. Late Monday afternoon he pulled out $5,000 in cash so he'd at least have something in case Preston decided the dance needed to start tonight. He'd also have his bank statements over the last year to show that he didn't have much beyond that.

At the end of the workday he went home.

The first thing he did was inspect the bed of the Tundra to see if there was any blood in there.

There was.

The raven-haired beauty had been in there.

She'd left her mark.

The number Rain scribbled on the matchbook was registered to one Rain DeVries. No Colorado driver's license pulled up for her, nor did a criminal record. The phone registration placed her at an address in an older part of Lakewood east of Alameda where the trees were big, the streets were crooked, and small ranches squatted on large lots.

Twilight settled over Denver.

The sky softened.

The heat dissipated.

Teffinger pulled the '67 into the woman's cracked asphalt driveway and killed the engine. A drainage ditch ran next to the property and gurgled against a quiet backdrop.

Crickets sang.

A startled garden snake disappeared under a bush.

No signs of life came from inside the house. The windows were closed, the door was shut and no lights or sounds were present.

Two newspapers were lying near the front door.

One was Sunday's.

The other was today's.

Teffinger knocked and got no answer. He tried the knob and found it wouldn't turn. Around back, the door was equally locked but one of the windows slid up when he tried it. After looking for nosy neighbors and seeing none, he slipped inside and closed the glass behind him.

"Anyone home?"

No one answered.

He was in a bedroom. The bed was made. He checked the closet and found it sardine tight with clothes, some sexy and some the opposite. In the first drawer of the nightstand was a vibrator and a 9mm Smith & Wesson. The second drawer was filled with bondage gear.

The top drawer of the dresser held panties and bras. They were the same style as the ones she was wearing Saturday night.

He headed deeper into the guts of the house.

The kitchen was old and cramped but clean. There was no indication that anything had been cooked or eaten or opened in the last two days.

A framed photo sat on the mantle in the living room. It showed Rain and an equally attractive female standing on a beach in bikinis with a large pier in the background. Teffinger wasn't sure, but he thought it might be the Santa Monica pier. He took it out of the frame and stuffed it in his back pocket.

A corner of the living room was converted to an office.

On a desk were bills and papers.

One of the stacks of bills was for her cell phone, six months deep, and matched the number she'd written on the matchbook. The statements didn't itemize ingoing and outgoing calls. All were paid except for the most recent one. Teffinger stuffed an older one in his pocket.

Another stack of bills was for Visa, again six months deep.

He grabbed the entire stack.

Inside the desk drawer was a checkbook, dating back six months, plus a pile of bank statements. He grabbed it all. A number of paycheck stubs were also in the drawer, going back six months. They were from the Majestic Casino & Hotel in Black Hawk. The amounts were minimal, suggesting she was more likely a cocktail waitress or money changer rather than a blackjack dealer.

There were no computers but an iPad was sitting on the desk.

He grabbed that too and then left.

He was weaving out of the neighborhood, almost to Alameda, when his cell phone rang and the voice of Preston came through.

"You got that pile all piled up yet?"

"You're blackmailing the wrong guy," Teffinger said. "I've got five grand and that's it."

"Five grand?"

"I have it in cash and you can have it tonight, right now if you want. That's all I have though."

"You want to buy your way out of a murder for five grand?"

"I'll show you my bank statements," Teffinger said.

Silence.

"Screw five grand and screw you. Get a hundred by this time tomorrow or pucker your lips and kiss your ass goodbye."

"How?"

"I don't know and I don't care. Borrow it, steal

it from an evidence box, I don't really give a shit. Just be damn sure you get it. This is your one and only chance."

The line went dead.

Teffinger headed home and bided his time until a solid darkness fell. Then he put a tarp and a shovel in the bed of the Tundra and headed for the warehouse district. If the silhouette on the floor turned out to be Rain's body, he'd bury it somewhere.

He'd testify at Zero's trial.

Preston's videotape showed Teffinger roughing up Rain and charging Preston with a broken beer bottle. It didn't show him actually killing Rain, however. That evidence could only be admitted through the testimony of the two witnesses, Preston and his girlfriend. Preston in turn was a blackmailer, so his credibility would be suspect. The girlfriend no doubt condoned the blackmail and would likely share the money, so she'd be equally suspect.

There was still a chance to take Zero down at trial.

The process would take Teffinger down as well but there was no getting around it. Either they'd both walk or both go down. Right now, Teffinger was leaning more towards the latter.

He parked a hundred yards short of the gap building and closed the distance on foot.

Noises came from inside the building, deep in the darkness. The closer Teffinger got, the more they sounded like animals feeding on something.

He got on the ground at the gap and pointed the flashlight inside.

Three good-sized dogs or coyotes were ripping a body apart.

They growled.

Their mouths pulled back.

Their fangs showed.

They were bloody.

The closest one let out a loud vicious bark and turned his body directly towards the light. The paws were firmly planted. The posture was low and tense. The eyes were yellow slits.

Teffinger slowly backed out.

Then he got the hell out of there.

DAY THREE

June 6
Tuesday

9

Silke Jopp, Esq. practiced law out of a three-story brick structure that started life at the turn of the century as a shoe factory. It sat at the edge of lower downtown Denver, LoDo, where the texture of the city was woven in shades of not-so-good art galleries, mom-and-pop restaurants and professional offices, mostly occupied by lawyers and architects and engineers who were more interested in parking and atmosphere than they were in a fancy financial district address.

The sign on the front door was small—Silke Jopp, P.C., Attorney-At-Law.

It belied the status of her reputation.

At a mere thirty-five years of age she was already the undisputed Queen of Defense, the attorney of choice for the affluent and powerful and the high-profile when the stakes were everything and the going was nasty.

She wasn't cheap.

Right now she was sitting on the building's back steps with a Camel dangling from her lips, dressed in her usual attire; jeans, Nike's and a plain blouse. Her hair was in a ponytail. A hop and jump down the alley, two magpies were scavenging through a dumpster.

Next week was the Decker Zero trial.

She was lucky to have the case.

Zero had first met with Bale Colton, Esq., out of New York, one of the only defense attorneys even more pronounced than her. After two short meetings a personality conflict developed.

Zero sought other counsel.

He landed in Silke's office.

The man had money enough to engage her services. Right now, she had an unlimited defense budget, with over a million dollars sitting in the retainer account.

Silke didn't know where Zero got his money.

She didn't care.

She knew it was green and that his checks cleared.

It was 10:10, meaning that in twenty minutes Neverly Cage would be coming by with her latest report. Inside, Silke's personal phone rang. She hesitated, deciding, then flicked the butt into the dirt and took the call.

A man's voice came through, one she didn't recognize.

"You don't know me," he said. "My name's Preston. I have some serious dirt on your star witness next week, Nick Teffinger."

Silke's heart pounded.

"What's your last name, Preston?"

"That's not important," he said. "What's important is that I have documentation of Teffinger doing something that you'll find very interesting."

"Such as what?"

"Such as killing a woman," Preston said. "Now let me cut to the chase. I'm looking for $500,000. That's the price and it's not negotiable."

Silke lit a cigarette. "Let's meet," she said.

10

Neverly Cage pushed through the front door of Silke's law office, still not sure whether she would be true to her employer and tell her about the dirt she got Saturday night on Teffinger or whether she'd be true to her promise to give him 48 hours.

Silke was out back in the alley, pacing with a Camel in her hand.

"Huge break," she said.

"Why, what happened?"

"I got a call from a mystery guy named Preston," Silke said. "He claims to have a cell phone video of Nick Teffinger killing a woman Saturday night."

The words hit Neverly with the force of a fist.

"How can that be?"

"The guy--Preston--was making out with a girlfriend down in the old warehouse district," she said. "Teffinger and some woman showed up. Teffinger tied her to a pole and then started to beat the shit out of her. The guy tried to get Teffinger to back off but Teffinger attacked him with a broken beer bottle."

"No way."

Silke smiled.

"The whole thing's on tape," she said. "A fight ensued and the guy got chased off. Teffinger thought he left but he didn't. The guy was still there and saw what happened next."

"Which is what?"

"Teffinger went back to the tied-up woman and slit her throat open with the beer bottle."

"Are you serious?"

Silke nodded.

"He wants five-hundred k for the tape. I already talked to Zero about it. He says to pay it and pay it fast."

Neverly tilted her head.

"Can you get it into evidence?"

Silke frowned.

"That's where it gets a little muddy," she said. "The guy tried to blackmail Teffinger but he didn't have any money. Then he read the paper this morning about the trial coming up next week and the fact that Teffinger was a key witness. He decided to forget about getting money out of Teffinger and get it out of me instead." She took a long drag, held it in and then blew out. "He says he'll come to court and authenticate the tape. Either him or his girlfriend or both of them."

"But he tried to blackmail Teffinger."

"Right, I know," Silke said. "He's not going to bring it up though, not on direct examination. The only way it will come up is if Teffinger brings it up. By that time, the tape will already be in evidence. Even if it's not in evidence yet, it will still come in. The blackmail part of the equation doesn't go to the authenticity of the tape. It only goes to the credibility of the man as to what he saw afterwards that didn't get on the tape." She smiled. "Actually, when you think about it, the blackmail part actually helps us as much as it hurts. It shows that the guy really did see the murder. Otherwise, he'd have nothing to blackmail Teffinger about."

Neverly nodded.

It made sense.

"Have you seen it yet?"

"No, but I will tonight," Silke said. "The guy says Teffinger's face is clearly visible and so is his truck, including the license plate. I can get an expert to testify that it hasn't been tampered with, assuming it hasn't." She sat down on the step and flicked the butt. Then she looked at Neverly and said, "So what have you turned up on your end? Anything?"

Neverly's blood pounded.

Teffinger murdered a woman.

Screw him.

"He was with a woman Saturday night at a club downtown called the D-Drop," she said. "I got pictures of them."

"Show me."

She did.

She showed her pictures of Teffinger getting sloppy drunk with a raven-haired beauty, letting his hands roam under the woman's short little sundress, then driving away drunk with her, and even sideswiping a car en route.

Silke smiled.

"These are golden," she said. "If the woman Teffinger tied up and killed is the same woman you have him documented with earlier in the evening, he's toast. We'll have his ass so nailed to the wall he won't be able to squirm an inch."

"There's more," Neverly said. "I followed him this morning. He went to a warehouse district and took a rope off a pole. Here's a picture of him doing it."

She pulled it up on her phone.

"Nice," Silke said.

"I didn't realize it at the time, but in hindsight he was obviously covering his tracks."

"What a little shit," Silke said. "It's going to be a lot of fun taking him down."

Neverly nodded.

"One more thing," she said. "He went into a

building a couple of blocks from the pole. When I showed up, he scrambled me out of there as fast as he could."

"Why was he in the building?"

"I don't know but I could guess."

Silke lit a cigarette.

"Nice day," she said. "Let's take a ride and see if there's a body in that building."

"You think?"

She nodded.

"Preston says Teffinger left with the woman in the bed of his pickup truck," she said. "He had to dump her somewhere. It would make sense that he wouldn't go far."

11

Silke and Neverly got to the warehouse district thirty minutes later and parked a hundred yards away so as to not leave any tire prints or other of scraps of evidence too close to the scene. Silke took one last drag on a Camel, mashed the butt in the ashtray and grabbed a flashlight from the back seat. Outside the beemer's air-conditioned oasis, a hot wasteland greeted them.

"This is it," she said.

"Yeah."

The roll-up delivery door had a two-foot gap at the bottom, exactly like it should.

Silke got her head down to ground level and shined the light in.

"Brace yourself. The smell isn't pretty."

She got flat on her stomach and edged her way inside.

Neverly followed.

Fifteen steps inside they found the horrific

remnants of a body that was now little more than bones and scraps of flesh. Gruesome bits and pieces were scattered in all directions as if they'd been ripped off by powerful jaws and dragged to where they could be devoured in peace.

The head was little more than a skull and gooey clumps of hair.

The face was totally eaten off.

The ears were gone.

Flies were everywhere, hundreds and hundreds, maybe thousands. As soon as Silke brushed one off her face, two more landed.

Neverly took twenty or thirty photos.

Then Silke said, "Let's get out of here."

Outside Silke studied the buildings across the street, particularly the upper levels. Then she headed for one, not the one directly across, the one just south of it and said, "Follow me."

"Why?"

"To find a place where you can videotape Teffinger responding to his own murder."

They entered through a broken rear window, using a rusty 55-gallon drum as a ladder. Enough light weaved in through cracks and holes to let them find an open stairway. They took it up four floors and made their way to the front of the building.

A pane of window glass was partially broken out, leaving a gap the size of a football.

"We'll position you right here," Silke said. "This side of the building is in the shade. From the outside, no one will see anything but darkness if they look up."

Neverly agreed.

"I'm starved," Silke said. "Let's get a bite. Then you can come back and set up. I'll make an anonymous call to the police regarding a body. Then we'll sit back and let them respond." She smiled. "God this is fun."

12

Tuesday afternoon Teffinger got a call from Barb Winters in dispatch to the effect that a body had been found down in the old warehouse district.

"Who found it?"

"From what I understand, some lady overheard two homeless guys talking about it. She didn't know if it was true or not but decided to make a call anyway and phoned it in to Precinct 9. They sent a patrol car over to sniff around and sure enough, there was a body. They said it's a mess. It looks like dogs got to it."

"Okay, I'm on it."

He swung by Sydney's desk.

"Field trip."

"A body?"

"Yeah," he said. "A messy one."

At the crime scene, Teffinger's palms sweated at

the sheer horror of the human carnage randomly disbursed on the concrete floor. He wiped them
on his pants and told Sydney, "I don't know what
killed her, but we'll treat it as a homicide if for no
other reason than she shouldn't be here."

"You think someone dumped her?"

"Either that or forced her here," he said. "I
want you take the lead."

The surprise on her face was palpable.

"Really?"

"That Decker Zero trial is going to be screwing
me up next week," he said. "It's time you took a
lead, anyway. You're ready."

"I take back half that stuff I said about you,"
she said.

"Only half?"

"That's more than fair."

He pointed the flashlight at a stairway and headed
up.

"Where you going?"

"Just to scout around."

That wasn't true.

He needed to clear his head. The woman's
blood was in the bed of his truck. Sure, he'd wiped
it down, but forensics could find it if they looked.
The broken beer bottle with the woman's blood
was in a plastic bag hidden deep in the guts of his
furnace room.

So was the rope.

So was the bloody button.

He got to the top floor. The windows were boarded with plywood. He peered out through a gap. Down below was the crime unit van, cop cars with lights flashing, crime scene tape, the coroner's van and people with serious faces; all there because of him.

Suddenly he saw something he didn't expect.

Across the street, a building down, someone in the upper level was behind a busted window pointing a camera at the scene. Teffinger looked harder and definitely detected movement. Who was it? A reporter? No car sat at the base of the building.

Teffinger headed down the stairs, out the back of the building and then down a full block until he was out of sight.

There he crossed the street.

Behind the buildings on that side was a weed-invested string of rusty tracks. He walked down the rails until he got to the building at issue.

On cat feet, he entered through a rear window and headed up.

On the top floor at the front of the building was a woman.

"Hi there," Teffinger said.

The head turned.

It belonged to Neverly Cage.

Her face was etched with stress. She took a step

back and said, "Don't hurt me."

He stopped.

"No one's going to hurt anybody. We're doing dinner tonight, remember?"

She shook her head.

"That's off."

"It is?"

"It's way off. I know what you did Saturday night after you left the D-Drop. So does Silke Jopp. A man named Preston has a videotape of the whole thing."

Suddenly his phone rang and the voice of Barb Winters came through from dispatch. "Got some more job security for you."

"You're kidding."

"Wish I was," she said.

"Where?"

"Up near Vasquez at the edge of a switchyard."

"What happened?"

"It's a woman," she said. "Someone stabbed her in the chest."

Teffinger got the exact location, confirmed he'd respond and directed his attention to Neverly.

"Is your car here?"

She nodded.

"It's down a couple of buildings."

"Why don't you give me a ride? We can talk on

the way."

"After you killed someone?"

He nodded.

"I'll pay the price for what I did," he said. "I'm not trying to get away with anything. But first I need to get Decker Zero behind bars."

13

The new crime scene wasn't as horrific as Rain's but was more than gruesome enough for Teffinger's taste. The victim was a woman in her mid to late twenties with long thick hair. She'd been beaten badly and stabbed in the heart with a large knife that was nowhere to be found. Most of her clothes had been cut off. By the looks of things she hadn't just been raped, but raped hard. It all took place at the remote end of an old BNSF switchyard near a silent string of broken boxcars. She'd been dead less than a day. The attack probably took place last night under the cloak of darkness.

She looked familiar.

Teffinger didn't know her but he'd seen her around; where or when he couldn't remember.

A search of the entire switchyard, all the way to the road, didn't turn up her purse. If she was chased to where she met her fate, she wasn't carrying her purse at the time. She didn't drop it in a panic.

Her shorts were ten steps from the body.

They were jeans material in the nature of Daisy Dukes.

Teffinger went through the pockets and found no car keys or identification. In the front pocket was a small amount of money, less than twenty dollars. In the back pocket, however, was something worth finding; a cell phone. Teffinger called his phone from hers, got the incoming number, and traced the registration to one D'aylor Alexander.

"What happened to you, D'aylor? Did some asshole spot your legs and decide he needed to have them?"

Teffinger called her phone from his and listened to the message.

Her voice was familiar.

He'd heard it somewhere.

He racked his brain trying to place it but got nothing other than more rack.

Processing the scene carried Teffinger into the early evening. En route home he called Sydney and said, "Did you get an ID on your body?"

"Negative."

"Did you run her prints?"

"I did. She didn't show up." A beat then, "You sound weird. What's going on?"

"Nothing."

A pause.

"Okay, be like that," she said. "Why don't I come over tonight? I'll bring some wine and pretend that everything you say makes sense."

He pictured it.

Ordinarily it would be perfect.

Tonight wouldn't be ordinary though.

He laid low. The heat morphed into twilight and the twilight morphed into night. At 9:45 he got in the '67, rotated the headlights up and pointed them towards downtown. He kept the radio off and reflected on his conversation with Neverly Cage this afternoon.

"You were seriously drunk," she said. "I don't think you would have killed her if you were sober."

"You got that right."

"Is that a defense, being drunk? Legally speaking, I mean."

He frowned.

"Not if it's self-induced."

She smiled.

"Well in that case you're SOL because you definitely spent more than a few hours inducing it." She grew serious and added, "You know, Teffinger, the power to make all this go away lies with you. It doesn't have to get ugly. Silke doesn't care about bringing you to justice. All she wants is a happy ending for Zero."

Teffinger studied her.

"What about you? Do you care about bringing me to justice?"

"I'll probably go to hell for it some day, but no," she said. "If your identification of Zero ends up getting fuzzy and the charges end up going away, you won't have to worry about me down the road. I'm not going to tell anyone what went down. I'm not going to blackmail you. Neither will Silke." She ran her fingers through his hair. "You can keep your job and bring twenty more Zero's to justice."

Teffinger pondered it.

"Tell me about the meeting between Preston and Silke," he said. "Where's it going to be? And when?"

"Silke's office, 10:30. You didn't hear it from me."

That was this afternoon.

Now it was night.

Teffinger parked the '67 in a lot with a guard not far from the stadium then took up a spot in the shadows across from Silke's building. There were three reserved parking spots directly in front of the entry. A silver 5-series BMW sat in one of them. The other two were empty.

It was 10:20.

The buzz and the bars were three blocks over.

Here the windows were dark and the streets were empty.

Headlights swung around a corner and punched this way. Teffinger wedged farther into the shadows and watched. An older model Ford F-150 pickup slowed as it passed. It was the same style and color as the one in the CD. A man was behind the wheel. His face was pointed at Silke's building as if scoping it out. A block later he turned to the right and disappeared.

"Come on, don't be afraid."

Two minutes later the vehicle returned.

This time it pulled next to the beemer and the lights went out. A man stepped out, briefly looked around, and then headed for the front door. It opened before he could knock. Silke came into view. She was dressed in jeans, a T and tennis shoes.

The man entered.

The door closed.

Teffinger's blood raced.

He waited a full minute and then another. He saw no one in either direction and then headed across the street with a GPS tracker in his right hand.

He slid under the back of the pickup being careful to not scald his flesh against the exhaust pipe and got the device securely fixed on the frame. He worked his way back out, looked at the license plate and memorized it.

Then he headed back into the shadows and scribbled the plate number onto the back of a business card.

Fifteen minutes later the door opened and Teffinger got his first good look at the man. He was average height, five-ten or thereabouts, with an equally average build—the kind of guy Teffinger could pound into oblivion at will. His lip was swollen and his left eye was black and blue, no doubt compliments of Teffinger's fists Saturday night. Teffinger had to admire the guy for interceding. He'd been up against a superior foe from the get-go.

A leather briefcase dangled from his right hand.

The deal had gone down.

14

Teffinger followed the GPS east on I-70 into a stinky neighborhood that sat down-wind of a dog-food manufacturing plant. Ironically the place wasn't too far from the BNSF switchyard where Teffinger spent most of the af-ternoon.

The truck was sold from one of those dubious dealerships on south Broadway six months ago. The license plate was registered to one Preston Lee.

Teffinger swung past the man's address and found the F-150 parked in the driveway. The inte-rior of the house was dark except for one upstairs light. That light was out the second time Teffinger swept past.

He parked down the street and killed the engine. Fire was in his veins.

His instinct was to bust in and teach the man a lesson about playing fast and loose with Teffinger's life. The gratification would be so extreme that it would almost be worth the consequences; almost, but not quite.

He let the thumping in his chest dim.

His eyes grew heavy.

He closed them, just to give them a moment of rest. It felt like climbing into a soft warm bed. He let them stay shut longer than he wanted.

"Ten more seconds," he told himself. "Just ten more."

He awoke some time later behind the wheel of the '67 with a serious crimp in his neck. His watch said 5:09 a.m. Every bone in his body was a limp noodle. His muscles were heavy and filled with mush. It was all he could do to get out of the car, wander over to the bushes and take a piss.

The air was cool.

Somewhere out in the darkness a dog barked.

It was for him.

He'd been warned.

Preston Lee's house was still dark but something was different. It took a moment before Teffinger finally realized what it was. The pickup truck was no longer in the driveway.

He zipped up and headed that way.

The doors and windows were locked but a sliding glass door to an upper-level deck off the upstairs bedroom was open. Teffinger muscled up a deck post and entered.

The briefcase wasn't in the first place he looked, under the bed. It was in the second place though, in the master closet, tucked behind a box.

He checked to be sure the money was still inside.

It was.

He took it and left.

DAY FOUR

June 7
Wednesday

15

Getting home shortly before dawn, Teffinger set the briefcase on the bed and counted the money, which was in denominations of twenties and fifties. To his amazement the full five hundred was in there. He expected only half that with the balance to come after trial. Apparently Silke wasn't as good a negotiator as her reputation suggested.

Preston was screwed.

He didn't have a single additional cent coming.

He'd probably think that Silke was somehow behind the theft. He'd figure that she had someone outside the office getting his license plate number while he was inside doing the deal. Maybe he'd figure she was following Zero's orders. Preston wouldn't suspect Teffinger. As far as he knew, Teffinger had no knowledge of who he was. The only way that could unravel is if Neverly told Silke that she told Teffinger about the time and place of the meeting and Silke figured it out from there and then told Preston what she thought happened. That probably wouldn't get into motion because there was no upside for Neverly to confess what she did. In fact, the opposite.

With any luck, the missing money would drive a wedge between Preston and Silke.

Sure, Silke still had the tape, but there was no murder on the tape. She needed Preston's testimony for that part of the story.

Teffinger divided the money into five equal piles, wrapped the piles in black plastic garbage bags, duct-taped the bags into tight rectangles and then hid them in the best locations he could find throughout the house.

Then he headed outside for a jog.

The specter of D'aylor Alexander's beaten and stabbed body at the switchyard shadowed his thoughts. The first thing he needed to do this morning was get over to her house and find out if anything there pointed towards her killer. He didn't have high hopes. His best guess was that she was randomly picked out on a spur-of-the-moment thing. The Daisy Dukes may have set the guy off.

Suddenly he realized something.

He'd heard her voice before and now remembered where.

She was the woman on Preston's tape, the

one in the background, the one whose face never showed. She was the one making out with Preston down in the warehouse district Saturday night when Teffinger kill Rain. He headed home and compared D'aylor Alexander's cell phone voice to the blackmail tape voice. There was no doubt that the two were the same.

So what happened? Did Preston kill her to cut her out of the money?

Did he make it look like a random sex attack so it wouldn't turn back on him?

That made sense. That would explain how the woman got lured to the switchyard. Preston probably told her they were just taking a walk. It would explain why she didn't have a purse with her.

Teffinger finished the run, showered, got into fresh clothes and headed for D'aylor Alexander's house in the '67 with a cup of coffee in his left hand and more of the same in a thermos.

Preston needed to go down.

He needed to go down hard.

He needed to go down forever.

D'aylor Alexander lived in a 3rd floor apartment slightly south of downtown on Broadway. Teffinger found a parking space for the '67 on the street between a gay movie arcade and a tattoo place called Ink You Up. He made sure the Vette was locked and headed over to the building. A sign on the elevator said Broken, which was fine because he wouldn't have entered it to escape a tarantula attack. He headed up the stairway, pushed through the door on the 3rd floor and got oriented. The apartment he wanted, 314, was to the right.

It was locked, as he expected.

It took ten minutes to round up the building manager, a guy in a wife-beater shirt named Bob who said, "She moved in about six months ago. I never had any trouble with her. She's quiet and pays on time. Her place is furnished which means that we own the furniture. It would be great if you didn't mess it up."

"Right."

Inside it was hot to the point of oppression.

Teffinger opened a window and turned on a fan. Since D'aylor was Preston's girlfriend, he expected to find pictures of the two them together. What he found instead was a photograph of D'aylor and Rain together.

They were on a beach, enjoying the day.

It was identical to the one he found in Rain's apartment.

At the BNSF crime scene, he had a feeling that he'd seen the victim before. Now he realized where that feeling came from. D'aylor was the other woman in the beach photo from Rain's apartment.

Suddenly his phone rang and a man's voice came

through. "Mr. Teffinger, I'm a lawyer and I need to speak to you right away. It's extremely urgent."

Teffinger didn't recognize the voice.

It came from a stranger.

"What's your name?"

"I'll tell you when we talk."

"Talk about what?"

"About a lot of things," the man said. "I'm in your living room right now. I'm waiting for you."

"Did you say you're in my living room?"

"Yes."

"This is a joke, right?"

"Let me put it this way," the man said. "You have a brick fireplace and the bricks are painted white. On the left side of the mantle you have four books laying flat. The top one has a red cover. The couch I'm sitting on is dark blue."

Teffinger's heart raced.

"How'd you get in?"

The man exhaled.

"That's not important," he said. "What's important is that we need to talk and we need to do it right now. I'm waiting for you. Come alone. Don't bring anyone with you. This needs to be private."

The line went dead.

Teffinger checked the number of the caller.

It was his home phone.

16

No vehicle was parked in Teffinger' driveway when he got home, which was unexpected if a lawyer was inside waiting for him. He'd left the front door closed and locked. Now it was open.

He entered.

The place was torn apart.

A large man in an expensive suit was leaning against the wall, sizing Teffinger up as he walked in. The guy was about Teffinger's age but at least two inches taller. He had black hair, slicked back, and a rough manly face with a square chin.

"Thanks for tearing my place apart," Teffinger said.

The man nodded.

"You're welcome. I think you know what I was looking for."

Teffinger feigned ignorance.

"I don't, but I do know one thing. Whatever

game it is that you're playing, it's a dangerous one."

The man shook his head as if disappointed.

"Don't screw with me," he said. "You don't have the skills and I don't have the time. I want the five hundred thousand and I want it now. Do that one simple thing and your little friend Neverly Cage will stay alive."

Neverly Cage.

An image of the woman's pretty face and innocent ways slammed into Teffinger's brain.

"You better not have—"

The man waved a hand and cut him off.

"She's fine and she's going to stay that way as long as you don't do anything stupid," he said. "Here's what's going to happen. You're going to give me the money and I'm going to tell you where she is. You can go get her and she won't end up rotting to death."

"She has nothing to do with anything," Teffinger said.

"On that count you're wrong," the man said. "She was the only one who knew about the meeting last night. She's been hanging around you. She told you about it."

"She didn't tell me anything."

The man frowned.

"She already confessed to it. You snuck over to Preston's and took the money. The briefcase is under your bed. That's a fact. It's also a fact that I want it back. Get it. Get it now. Do you understand?"

"Who are you?"

"Just get the money." The man pulled a gun and pointed it at Teffinger's chest. "You have one minute."

Teffinger exhaled.

"Sure, no problem."

With the man in tow and the gun at his back, Teffinger pulled the five stashes out of their hiding places and handed them over.

The man put them in the briefcase and said, "See, that wasn't so hard."

"Your turn," Teffinger said. "Where's Neverly?"

The man cocked his head.

"It would be hard to explain. I'll take you to her." He pulled a pair of handcuffs out of his jacket pocked and tossed them. "Put these on, behind your back."

Teffinger balked.

"We can go get her or she can rot to death," the man said. "If she rots, though, the blood's on your hands. You had your chance and didn't take it."

Teffinger's phone rang.

The man said, "Cuffs first."

Teffinger hesitated, bit his lower lip and complied.

The man said, "Don't to anything stupid." Then he connected the incoming call and put the phone between his ear and Teffinger's.

"This is Teffinger."

"Nick, it's me."

The voice belonged to a woman.

It was familiar but he couldn't place it.

"Who is this?"

"It's me, Rain."

Rain?

Rain was dead.

"Where are you?"

"At home."

"I'm coming over," she said. "We need to talk. A friend of mine was killed, a friend named D'aylor Alexander. I know who did it. It was a guy named Bale Colton. He's a lawyer out of New York."

"How do you know?"

"Just stay there. I'll be there in fifteen minutes."

The line went dead.

Teffinger looked at the man.

"Is that your name, Bale Colton?"

The man nodded.

"Is what she said true? Did you kill D'aylor Alexander?"

The man frowned.

"Well, this is a conversation I never expected to have," he said. "It's strange how life works some-times, isn't it?"

17

The man made Teffinger sit on the couch as he paced in front of him, far enough away that a leg couldn't kick out or a sudden move could get him. At first he said nothing and checked his watch every fifteen seconds. Then he said, "I didn't want it to end this way. I didn't want to have to kill you. It's ironic that the ending is going to be what it's going to be because if I was going to kill you, things would have been a whole lot simpler from the start."

Teffinger's chest pounded.

He was going to die.

"Let's work it out," he said.

The man shook his head.

"How can we work it out now that you know I killed D'aylor Alexander?"

"It'll be our secret. I'll misdirect the case and then close the file."

"Sure."

Teffinger exhaled.

"Why'd you kill her? What'd she ever do to you?"

"It's complicated."

"What isn't?"

The man nodded.

He sat down in a chair facing Teffinger and leaned forward. "I guess it's only fair that you know. I'm Decker Zero's attorney."

"I thought Silke Jopp was his attorney."

"She is," the man said. "She's his second attorney. I'm his first attorney."

"I don't get it."

"Zero's a very wealthy man," he said. "I met with him early on and we devised a plan to discredit the people's main witness."

"Me," Teffinger said.

"Right, you. The plan was for you to kill someone. To distance both Zero and myself from the plan, we pretended to have a falling out. He then hired Silke Jopp who had no idea that things were at work behind the scenes. Rain and Preston and D'aylor Alexander were all part of the plan."

"How?"

"It was simple," he said. "We've done this before, eight times before to be exact. The three of them moved to Denver six months ago."

Six months ago.

"Why?"

"So they'd be living in town when the kill took place," she said. "We monitored your moves. You went to D-Drop every other Friday."

Teffinger cocked his head.

That was true.

"Rain picked you up," he said. "She got you drunk and slipped you some drugs. She took you to a deserted warehouse district—a place recommended by Zero, in fact. She pretended to find abandoned rope on the ground. It was already staged there. She talked you into tying her up against a pole."

"So that was her idea?"

"Yes it was," he said. "She told you she liked it rough. She told you to slap her around and rip her clothes off. You were real hesitant about that part but she kept pounding on you and you finally did it. Preston was in the shadows videotaping the whole thing. He interceded and that's where the camera stopped rolling, ostensibly dropped. What happened after that is that Preston subdued you easily. He injected you with a form of roofies. Then he drove you home in your truck and moved you behind the wheel."

Teffinger shook his head.

"And you all got paid handsomely by Zero," he said.

"Yes we did," the man said. "The beauty is that Silke Jopp and her little investigator, Neverly Cage, thought the whole thing was real. That way they could get passionate at trial in a way that I wouldn't have been able to, knowing the truth."

"Clever."

"Thanks."

"What I don't get is why you killed D'aylor?"

The man exhaled.

"She got greedy," he said. "She was shaking me down. Like I said, we did eight similar cases before this one. She was in on all of them. She looked back at the whole thing and didn't think she'd been paid properly. She wanted more money, a lot more money, otherwise she was going to spill her guts to all the wrong people."

"Why didn't you just pay her?"

"You know why," he said. "Once they start to turn you can't trust them any more. Like I said before, we could have just killed you at the outset. That would have been a lot easier than going to all the effort we did. With you dead the state's case would have fallen apart. We try to not kill anyone unless it's absolutely necessary."

"But still, you do."

He nodded.

"Occasionally, but only as a last resort."

"So how many times have you killed?"

"Not that many," he said. "Three. That will go up to five with you and Rain. In hindsight, Rain must have known D'aylor was shaking me down.

She knew that I had a motive. Hell, for all I know she was even in on the blackmail. Maybe they had plans to split the money."

Teffinger tugged quietly at the cuffs.

They cut into his flesh.

They were tight.

They weren't coming off.

"I'll make a deal with you," he said. "You killed D'aylor. There's no way you can undo that and there's no way I can forget what I know. We can make an exchange though. I can give you a pass on D'aylor as long as you let Rain go."

"So you'd be giving up a catch to save a future victim? That's how you're looking at it—"

"Right."

The man shook his head.

"It won't work."

"Why not?"

"Because what you'd do is get Rain safe, then come after me. Tell me I'm wrong."

Teffinger looked into the man's eyes.

His mouth opened to speak but no words came out.

Suddenly a sound came from the kitchen.

"Hey, Bale."

The man turned, froze for a heartbeat and then jerked for his gun.

A shot rang out.

The man's face exploded.

He teetered for a second and then slumped forward into the carpet.

He didn't move.

His eyes were open, looking at nothing.

Rain lowered her arm.

She studied the man's body as if in a trance, then set a gun down on the table and looked at Teffinger.

TWO WEEKS

LATER

Saturday

18

The cruise in Golden was one of the largest in the country. Once every month on a Saturday night, from the Sonic at one end all the way down to the high school at the other, an otherwise ordinary stretch of city asphalt became home to thousands and thousands of the best vehicles the '50s and '60s and '70s had to offer. Modern muscle was also welcome and made an appearance in the shape of Chargers, Vipers, Mustangs and even an occasional Porsche. Every conceivable parking space up and down the road was jammed with vintage.

The sidewalks were lined with lawn chairs and bodies in motion.

Throaty engines revved.

Tires squealed.

Right now the late-day shadows were long but the air still burned with the afternoon's fire.

Teffinger was in the '67 with the top down,

making his third pass, sandwiched between a '69 Camaro in front and a '57 Chevy behind. Neverly was in the passenger seat wearing oversized sunglasses and a tattered cap turned backwards. Down below was a short green skirt and strong legs that Teffinger still hadn't fully opened.

They were taking things slow.

A lot had happened in the last two weeks.

For starters, Rain's bullet to Bale Colton's head was ruled to be self-defense.

Decker Zero's trial didn't go well, for Zero that is. Teffinger returned the five hundred k to Preston with the understanding that Preston would in turn return it to Silke, which he did. The videotape defense that Teffinger killed Rain was gone, given the troubling little fact that Rain was still breathing and walking around the earth in feet that weren't dead. Even the pictures Neverly took of Teffinger at the D-Drop weren't used as evidence at trial. That was because the state could call Rain as a rebuttal witness to testify that she orchestrated the whole evening, all as part of a bigger plan—known to and even paid for by the defendant, Zero—to falsely attempt to discredit Teffinger by pinning a fake murder on him. In the end, the jury found Teffinger's eyewitness testimony to be credible and convicted Zero on all counts.

Sentencing would take place next month.

The smart money was on life without parole.

It wasn't enough but it was something.

In exchange for immunity, Rain and Preston were cooperating with authorities across the country. So far, six defendants who walked following tainted trials had been rearrested on new charges of obstruction of justice.

It was still unclear who the dead woman was that got torn apart by the dogs. Teffinger's best theory was that the murder was connected to the woman Zero killed. The area was being used to release women naked and then hunt them down.

Traffic ahead came to a stop.

Teffinger shifted into neutral and put on the brakes.

Neverly said, "It's hot out."

Teffinger nodded.

"Yeah."

Neverly scooted her dress up and fanned her legs. A black thong came into view.

"I wore this for you," she said.

"The thong?"

She spread her knees ever so slightly.

"No, the body. Tonight, it's yours, assuming you want it."

He put his hand on her thigh.

"I don't want it, I want you," he said.

She looked at him with a serious face and then

broke out in laughter.

Teffinger smiled.

"Okay," he said. "Busted. It's the body I want."

"You were gone there for a second."

He raked his hair back with his fingers.

"I was but I'm back now. It won't happen again."

"I hope not."

Formerly a longstanding trial attorney before taking the big leap and devoting his fulltime attention to writing, RJ Jagger (that's a penname, by the way) is the author of over twenty hard-edged mystery and suspense thrillers. In addition to his own books, Jagger also ghostwrites for a well-known, bestselling author. He has been a member of the International Thriller Writers since 2006.

RJJagger.com